There was something between Lynn and White Moon that came close to being magic. White Moon's smooth rhythm turned a fiery performance into a thing of grace and beauty that brought the audience to its feet. Lynn had dressed in white, and her pale hair streamed free behind her as she lifted her hat to acknowledge the applause.

Mounted on his stallion, Bryan watched. Others might have seen the perfect union between horse and rider, but Bryan saw only the slender young woman. He thought he could be detached, that he would be able to see nothing more than an athlete when he looked at Lynn. But then his heart came undone.

He wanted her. He wanted her body and mind, but most of all Bryan wanted Lynn's heart.

ABOUT THE AUTHOR

Vella Munn has a long-standing interest in rodeos. The idea for *White Moon* came while she was traveling through high prairie country on her way home from her stepfather's funeral. Thinking of that man, a onetime rodeo cowboy and working cowboy who'd given her mother ten years of companionship and love, Vella knew she had to share her feelings about that life-style and the special people who embrace it. Vella Munn lives and works in Jacksonville, Oregon.

Books by Vella Munn
HARLEQUIN AMERICAN ROMANCE

42–SUMMER SEASON
72–RIVER RAPTURE
96–THE HEART'S REWARD
115–WANDERLUST
164–BLACK MAGIC
184–WILD AND FREE
264–FIREDANCE

Don't miss any of our special offers. Write to us at the following address for information on our newest releases.

Harlequin Reader Service
901 Fuhrmann Blvd., P.O. Box 1397, Buffalo, NY 14240
Canadian address: P.O. Box 603,
Fort Erie, Ont. L2A 5X3

WHITE MOON

VELLA MUNN

Harlequin Books

TORONTO • NEW YORK • LONDON
AMSTERDAM • PARIS • SYDNEY • HAMBURG
STOCKHOLM • ATHENS • TOKYO • MILAN

To the memory of Bob Palmer

Published August 1989

First printing June 1989

ISBN 0-373-16308-8

Chapter One

Night's shadows still clung to the corners of the corral when Lynn Walker opened the gate and stepped
inside. The gelding at the far end of the enclosure
snorted. For a moment the Levi's-and-shirt-clad
young woman just leaned against the fence.

Lynn Walker could have waited until later in the day
for what she planned to do, but she had wakened early
and, not wanting to disturb her mother, had dressed
and left the ranch house. Now that she was here, she
might as well settle the question of what to do about
Red.

Cautiously Lynn started toward the animal. The
movement brought her out of the shadows, highlight-
ing the contrast between tanned flesh and flaxen hair.
She held the coiled rope behind her, talking softly the
way she'd talked to a thousand horses in her twenty-six
years. "Don't like me very much, do you, big Red?"
she droned. "Never have been crazy about humans,
have you? All they've done is clean you off when you
were born, pull you through a siege of colic, feed you
and try to put a saddle on your back."

As if he knew the meaning of the word "saddle,"
the Roman-nosed roan snorted again. This time the

blast from his nostrils made the long, sensitive hairs on his muzzle quiver.

"That's the whole problem, isn't it?" Lynn continued, measuring her forward progress in inches. "Something between your ears gets bent out of shape when someone tries to tighten a cinch around you. Your mother was the same way." Lynn laughed softly, remembering. "Boy, did she give me the evil eye when I tried to break her. She won that round. I was the one who wound up with a broken arm."

Red stared intently as Lynn came closer, but the gelding only flattened his ears when she put a warm hand on his neck. Lynn felt the power beneath her fingers.

"You were a magnificent yearling," Lynn informed the horse. "All satin and sleek hair stretched over a frame that never stopped moving." Lynn kept talking until Red's ears pricked forward, then she produced the rope. Red dropped his head to sniff the new hemp and then snorted. Still he didn't whirl away. Slowly Lynn reached up and slipped the rope around his powerful neck. "Come on, Red. Show me you haven't turned out as bad as Mom says you have."

Red went with Lynn when she pulled on the rope. Back at the gate was the saddle and bridle Lynn had brought out of the barn for the test. "It's not so bad is it?" she asked in the same low droning tone as the skittish horse's unshod hooves landed inches from her size five boots. His shoulder jarred her slim frame as woman and animal made momentary contact, but Lynn felt no fear. She respected a horse's strength and unpredictability. But fearing horses wasn't part of her makeup.

"Maybe it wouldn't be like this if I'd been around to give you some gentling when you needed it. I'm sorry. Things don't always turn out the way we want them to." She couldn't help but think the two years she'd been away would have been better spent here.

Lynn warmed the cold metal of the bit in her hands before trying to work it between the gelding's teeth, then slipped the leather bridle into place. "Now for the s-a-d-d-l-e," she spelled, her eyes never leaving the horse's eyes. "I wish Nevada Girl was here. She'd show you a thing or two about manners."

Red's eyes were on the saddle. Wise in the ways of horses, Lynn didn't turn her back on the gelding who was now pawing the ground. "Don't give me a hard time," she continued as she let the animal run his lips over the saddle horn. "There's no place for you here if you put up a fuss about being ridden."

Finally, Lynn took a breath and held it. "This is it," she warned both the horse and herself. Then she swung the saddle up and onto Red's high back.

Red snorted and shied away, not stopping until he was pinned against the fence. Only when the loose flesh on his back stopped twitching did she release the cinch so that it hung below Red's belly. She reached under and grabbed; Red kicked at his belly as she tightened the saddle.

Lynn shook the horn to make sure the saddle was secure and then untied the snubbing rope. She planted her foot in the stirrup before the horse knew he was free. Her whole being was focused on the simple yet dangerous act of swinging herself into the saddle.

Straddling a potential keg of dynamite was something Lynn had done enough times that she no longer questioned her sanity. There was nothing left of her but energy and muscles and courage. She wanted this. No, she *needed* this!

Her jeans had barely made contact with the saddle when Red tucked his head between his legs and flung both hind legs out behind him. She let the reins slide through her hands to keep from being jerked off and clamped Red's sides with thighs muscled by a lifetime spent on horseback.

Red pawed for the sky. When the big horse landed, the jolt was almost enough to send Lynn into the dirt. Still she held on, teeth rattling every time the animal bucked. Red wasn't going to win this round!

Suddenly he changed tactics and raced full speed toward the far end of the corral. Lynn threw her head back and let loose a rebel yell into the cold morning air. "Go Red! Run me into the ground!"

Inches before he would hit the fence, Red skidded to a stop, his haunches dropping nearly to the ground. If she could have been sure Red would whirl and re-trace his pounding steps, Lynn would have stayed with the rogue. But she'd mounted the horse to learn one thing, and her answer had come with Red's first move. This wasn't an animal for Walker Ranch.

Before Red could collect himself, Lynn catapulted herself out of the saddle, grabbed the wooden fencing and scrambled over it. It wasn't until she was on the ground with a barrier between herself and the still enraged horse that she took her first conscious breath.

"Red! You damn fool!" Lynn called after the bucking animal. "You're just like me. Fighting a rope even when you don't know why you're fighting." Lynn took another breath. At least Red knew what he was battling. Lynn couldn't name what it was that had once caused her to search the horizon with hungry eyes.

"Lynn Walker! I should have known. Are you hurt?"

Lynn turned at the sound of her mother's cry. The older Walker woman, wearing a nightgown that hung loosely on her too thin figure, was closing the distance between the ranch house and the corral. Like her surroundings, Carol Walker was gray. Timeless. Briefly Lynn closed her eyes. She hadn't wanted to disturb her mother. The woman was bone weary and might be for months to come. "I'm fine," she said. "I just wanted to give Red one last chance."

"Do you have any idea how many chances that rogue has had?" Carol Walker took her daughter's arm and turned her slim but muscled form around. "What he is is rodeo stock."

Lynn didn't bother looking at the horse before nodding. "Do you want to call them or shall I?"

"Why don't you call Dee, dear? You haven't gotten in touch with her since you came back, have you?"

"No." Lynn thought about using a lack of time as her excuse but dismissed the lie. Dee was her best friend and Lynn had had ample opportunity to tell her that her father's funeral had accomplished what both Dee and Carol had wanted—Lynn was back.

"Dee said I'd hitch a ride back here someday," Lynn said softly. "I guess it's time she learned how right she was. Is her father still involved with the ranch and business?"

Carol shook her head and rearranged her nightgown over her angular shoulders. "You know Bob. He was always full of ideas. He just never had much knack for seeing them through. It's a good thing

Bryan took to contracting the way he did. He's been running things close to ten years now."

Bryan. The name of her best friend's older brother didn't come easily. While Dee had always been like a friendly kitten, warming instantly to everyone she met, Bryan was the wind that moved the prairie grasses. Lynn had known Bryan Stone from earliest childhood, and yet she'd never understood the man; she wondered if anyone did.

Lynn broke free of her thoughts. "I've seen Stone stock at half the rodeos I've been to. I take it he's doing well."

"More than well. Stone stock has been at the finals for what, the past seven years at least. Bryan knows his animals. And he's a businessman."

Lynn pulled away from the fence and focused on the rising sun. "Is he married? Dee always said no woman could ever get close enough to throw a rope on him."

"He's still running wild. Poor Nancy. I think she's worried she's never going to have grandchildren. Dee's having too much fun being single and Bryan... If Bryan ever stands still for more than five minutes, he's going to make some woman a good husband. I didn't tell you at the funeral but—" Carol swallowed and then continued. "Bryan was here the day your dad died. Sick as he was, William wanted to talk to Bryan."

"What about?" When the family gathered for the funeral two weeks ago, Carol hadn't yet been able to talk about her husband's last days. That release, which Lynn knew was essential, was just now starting to come.

"Maybe nothing." Carol shrugged. "Bryan was going to go to an auction that day, but when your dad called, he dropped everything and came over."

"The Stones have always been good neighbors. More like family."

"I know." Carol's voice dropped to a whisper. For a minute Lynn thought she wasn't going to say anything else. "Honey, your father died in Bryan's arms. I—I don't know what I was thinking that day. I let Bryan and your father talk me into running some errands while Bryan stayed here. It'd been so long since I'd had any time... When I came back, there was nothing to do except hold his hand and tell him goodbye."

"Oh, Mom!" Lynn embraced her mother, hiding her own tears in the older woman's gray hair. A thousand regrets, all coming too late, pounded through her.

"Don't," Carol warned in a shaky whisper. "You had no idea your dad was that sick. Even with the trouble with his lungs, I thought he was going to live forever. I—I'm just glad you're here now. But honey..." Carol pulled her back until she was looking deep into the earth-green eyes that had once seemed too big for her face and were still her most commanding feature. "I don't want you staying here out of a sense of obligation. You were making a life for yourself."

The small cabin that went along with her less than satisfying job at one of the top barrel racing schools outside Phoenix wasn't much. "You're not going to get rid of me that easily, Mom," Lynn said, tossing her head. "Some of us—" she paused. "Some of us take longer to get on the right track. Bryan has always had goals. Always been so sure what he wanted out of life. That's what drove Dee crazy about him."

"They're still squabbling like a couple of kids." Carol smiled faintly. "They remind me of you and your brothers. You're sure about Red?"

"I'll call as soon as we get back to the house. Red's meant for the rodeo circuit."

"I know." Carol sighed. "I think your father had already decided to sell him before." Carol shook her head angrily. "I let William protect me too much. Red should be off earning his keep. I could have done that much."

"Don't," Lynn warned her mother gently. "You've had enough to do without worrying about that hay burner. What do you mean Dad protected you? Who's the one who convinced Dad to try a wheat crop? It worked didn't it? Besides, those brothers of mine will be lighting back here soon," Lynn said. "It's about time those two earned *their* keep."

A stronger smile touched Carol's face. "Now, that sounds familiar. I've lost count of how many fights I had to referee between you and your brothers. I certainly hope that's not going to start again."

"I'll act civilized around Chet," Lynn conceded. "Big brother's downright stodgy these days. But you can't expect things to change between Bullet and me. It's your own fault, you know. You set the stage by having me just thirteen months after Bullet. And I still say he locked me in that horse trailer overnight on purpose."

At thirty, Chet had a wife and two small children. They'd been living in the southern part of the state while Chet managed an auction, but the auction land had recently been sold for some kind of development

and it made sense for him to come back and take over
the family business. Twenty-seven-year-old Dave, or
Bullet, as everyone called him, was a bronc riding
cowboy who thought of nothing except once again
making it to "The Finals," as the world series of rodeoing was called. This time of year, Bullet wouldn't
be able to take much time off the circuit, but Lynn
knew that the presence of her youngest and wildest
son, even if only for a few days, would do a great deal
to boost Carol Walker's spirits.

Lynn accompanied her mother back into the cool,
clean house. She waited until Carol went into her
bedroom and then reached for the phone, dialing the
Stone number from memory. For a moment, she felt
like a teenager calling her best friend to see if Dee was
free to work on the trick riding act that had made them
a popular local attraction.

But it wasn't Dee Stone who answered the phone.

"Lynn? I didn't know you were back. Is your
mother all right?"

"My mother's fine," Lynn explained. "As for my
reasons for being back...it's a long story. You can use
a good bucker, can't you? Are you interested in Red?"

"The question is, are you sure you're ready to do
this?" Bryan asked, his tone gentle. "You're the one
who dried him off."

So Bryan Stone remembered the ties between her
and Red. Lynn hadn't expected that. "No one's been
able to take the bronc out of him. He's a rogue, Bryan.
He's right for bucking stock. Do you want to take a
look at him?"

Bryan was silent for a moment. "I have to be out
your way this afternoon, Lynn. What if I drop by
then?"

Bryan was still as decisive and fast acting as always. "That'll be fine. Is Dee there? I'd love to talk to her."

"She's out with the vet. But if I tell her you're at the ranch, I know she'll come with me. Lynn, how is your mother? I haven't talked to her since last week."

"She's coping. She's a strong woman, Bryan. I think it'll be better once she gets over being so tired."

"She ran herself into the ground looking after your dad. Your mother's a remarkable woman, Lynn."

Lynn closed her eyes, concentrating. She couldn't remember ever having a personal conversation with Bryan Stone. "Mom wasn't expecting Dad to die so soon," Lynn said softly, honestly. "None of us were."

"Your dad knew he couldn't fight emphysema forever, Lynn." Bryan's voice dropped to a whisper that matched her own. "He was tired. At least the end came quickly."

Thank God, Lynn acknowledged, although she didn't have the courage to speak the words aloud. "Thank you for being there," she said instead.

"I'll never be sorry it worked out that way. I didn't want them to be alone."

With those few words, Bryan put an end to Lynn's hope that they might be forging a relationship that hadn't been possible when they were younger. *She* should have been the one to make those last days easier for her parents. She, not a neighbor, should have been the strong one.

"Is around four in the afternoon all right?"

"Fine," she replied woodenly. "Four it is."

Lynn stood staring at the silent receiver, her eyes behind their thick curtain of lashes darkening. Bryan had always been short on talk; their conversation today might well hold a record for them. She wondered if he knew that in the space of a few words, he'd pulled her guilt out and made her face it.

And thrown it back at her.

Chapter Two

Bryan Stone sat behind the wheel of the four-wheel drive pickup he'd put 20,000 miles on in the last six months. His left arm hung out the open window, the afternoon sun unable to add anything to flesh weathered by a lifetime spent outdoors. As usual he was waiting for his sister, this time for the trip out to the Walker ranch.

Today Bryan wasn't glancing impatiently at the house. He was staring over the flat expanse of his land, which was punctuated by barbed wire fences and dotted with livestock. A stranger to the ranch would need an explanation for the coexistence of two-thousand pound Brahma crossbreds, big bodied horses with feet the size of dishpans and long-horned steers too tough for any pot. Bryan's explanation would be short and simple. This was how he made his living.

But Bryan wasn't thinking about that. The phone call from Lynn Walker had taken him back to a scene that had been played out a couple of weeks before. Both Bryan and William Walker had known the end was coming. Once Carol was out of the house, William had put aside his pretense of having called Bryan over to discuss business and they talked for a little while about William's family, particularly his daughter, Lynn.

After that, the two men said little. Bryan didn't know how long he'd been sitting in the oddly darkened living room when, for the first time in years, William wasn't pulling for air.

That day Bryan Stone learned something precious about a time for living and a time for dying. He'd said goodbye to an old friend. What else he learned in the too-quiet house he kept to himself, because for Bryan, words like escape and pain and responsibility didn't come easy. He could feel them; he just couldn't say them.

"I'm ready," Dee announced as she bounced onto the high seat. "Did I disturb your daydreams?"

"I was just thinking. Look, I don't have much time," he explained as he maneuvered the truck onto the gravel driveway leading toward the county road. "I have to get into town before the feed store closes. You can catch up with Lynn later."

"In other words, no gossiping." Dee jabbed her brother playfully. "But Bryan, do you think she's here for good? I mean, she came for the funeral, and now she's back again. I knew she'd made a mistake taking off two years ago with what's his name."

Bryan let his sister rattle on. It would make her happy to have her old friend back, but if she and Lynn started running around together, Bryan couldn't help wondering if Dee's newfound dedication to the family business wouldn't go out the window. Two women chasing the wind was more trouble than he needed.

Dee's snort told Bryan he'd been caught. "You aren't listening, are you? You, big brother, are hopeless."

"Just tuning out the background noise," Bryan offered. "You've yet to say anything important."

"Oh, yeah? Would you like to hear how much it cost us when that truck broke down out of Redding? Having to transfer the broncs to a rental cost plenty. We still have to find a new engine and *pronto*."

Bryan grunted.

"One problem at a time." Bryan tightened his grip as the truck bounced over ruts. "The handler I had to fire last week—Dak Davies— Did he get his final paycheck?"

"You better believe it." Dee shook her head. "He was as mad as I've ever seen anyone. You're on his hit list, you know."

"Me and everyone he's ever been in contact with. He didn't give you too much of a hard time, did he?"

Dee winced as the left rear tire hit a chuckhole. "Nothing I couldn't handle."

Financial discussions filled the time until they'd covered the remaining few miles separating the two ranches that were Harney county landmarks. Up until a year ago, Bryan had employed a local woman as bookkeeper for Stone Stock, but then the woman had decided to go to college. To Bryan's considerable surprise, Dee had quit her job with the extension service and taken over the business's books. It might have taken Dee Stone longer to decide what she wanted to do with herself than Bryan figured it should, but he had no complaints with the way she handled her job. Bryan glanced at his sister. What would the result have been if their personalities had blended a little? Dee might have grown up realizing there was more to life than fun and laughter. And perhaps he would have taken time for boyhood.

But it hadn't been like that. Eighteen-hour days, far from exhausting him, kept Bryan Stone in peak form both physically and emotionally. The rare moments of riding into the arena as part of the opening ceremony, straw bossing the behind-the-chutes operations, being the one everyone turned to for direction during the fast-paced hours while a rodeo was underway, that was what made the blood pound in his veins.

And yet even those moments paled in comparison to riding along the high prairie land at the east end of the ranch, a good horse under him, early morning air whipping his face.

LYNN WAS RIDING NEVADA GIRL near the county road, looking over the crop of spring lambs, when the pickup hauling a horse trailer bearing the words Stone Stock pulled into the earthen driveway. Dee Stone was leaning out of the passenger's side window. "You're back! Please tell me you're back for good!"

"I'm back you fool. You're going to get yourself killed!" Lynn yelled as she pulled Nevada Girl alongside the now motionless truck.

"I'm glad you came with Bryan," Lynn finished. "We have so much to talk about."

"Did you think I wouldn't come? I have so much to tell you. Do you remember the Harper boy? He—"

"Not now," Bryan interjected. "There isn't time. You can talk later."

"Nag, nag, nag," Dee shot back. "I hope you get an ulcer. Is that Nevada Girl? From the way you're sitting her, I'd never know you two had ever been separated.''

Lynn moved closer, hoping for a clearer view of her friend. But it wasn't Dee who caught her attention. From where she sat on Nevada Girl, Lynn could make out little except a masculine profile, dark at the jaws, as if the man's whiskers defied whatever he used for shaving. His thick eyebrows were as dark as his jet hair. His shoulders were so broad they dwarfed the steering wheel, which he gripped with his callused hands. Anything she might have said died in her throat as Bryan Stone turned his coal-black eyes in her direction.

Lynn should have been prepared for those eyes; she'd seen him enough times. But she'd never known a man whose eyes went as deep or probed as intently as Bryan's did.

Dee and Bryan Stone's grandmother had been a Kiowa Indian. Dee took after the English side of the family with blue eyes and light brown hair accenting her fine features, but Bryan's high cheekbones and firm mouth were a legacy from the tribe that called the Black Hills their home. Lynn believed that his Kiowa ancestors were still living in those eyes.

''We better do as he says,'' Dee said, breaking the silence. ''You know Bryan. He's always on a tight schedule unless he's out on one of his predawn rides. Where's that bronc of yours?''

Lynn pointed in the direction of the corral to the left of the barn. ''I'll join you in a minute,'' she said, backing Nevada Girl with a practiced hand so that she wouldn't have to breathe the dust kicked up by the truck's big tires.

Lynn watched the vehicle bounce down the road. Dee and Bryan had aged a couple of years, but unlike Nevada Girl, they hadn't grown too old for the lifestyle they'd inherited at birth.

With her free hand, Lynn caressed her mare's silken neck. "I might be looking for another mare, old girl, one with more speed and durability. But there'll always be a home for you here. There'll never be another horse with your heart."

Dee had jumped out of the truck and was bouncing up and down, impatient to have Lynn reach them. Lynn noticed that she still wore her jeans skintight. "How is Nevada Girl doing?" Dee called out.

Lynn pulled her horse to a stop and swung out of the saddle. "She still favors that right front leg." She thought for a moment, then added, "You don't know anyone who's selling a good horse, do you?"

"Do you know what an experienced barrel racing horse goes for these days?" Dee asked. "You could get a luxury car for that kind of money."

"I didn't say anything about competing," Lynn corrected her friend. "You're getting ahead of me."

"Am I?" Dee asked. "You were always better than me. You could go on the circuit again, you know."

"I could?" Lynn was only barely aware that she'd asked the question aloud.

Bryan joined the women, his dark eyes taking in a great deal. "Don't get another barrel racer unless you're sure you're going to compete," he said softly. "Don't cage up an animal that's bred to run."

Bryan was right. But then he usually was when it came to animals. "I wouldn't do that. I'd love to give competing a shot, but I'm not sure how practical that is," she answered honestly. "There're a lot of things I have to decide now that I'm back."

"You really are back?" Dee grabbed Lynn's wrists. "For good, I mean? Oh, that's wonderful. At least I hope it's wonderful for you."

Lynn hugged Dee, looking over her friend's shoulder to her silently watching brother. "I hope I can give you the answer to that before long. The truth is, I'm not sure. I thought I knew what I was doing when I went back to Phoenix after Dad's funeral, but the moment I walked into my rental I knew I couldn't stay there. It was like... Oh never mind. What do you think?" Lynn brightened. "Do you think we're too old to impress people with our trick riding routines?"

"I think I've forgotten most of them," Dee admitted as she released her friend. "Lynn, we haven't done those since we were kids."

"Pretty ignorant kids." Bryan hadn't taken his eyes off her, yet there was nothing critical in his observation.

"It's a wonder we weren't killed considering some of the stunts we pulled," Lynn went on. "Do you remember when we were on that big chestnut quarter horse of yours and the reins snapped? I thought we were never going to get that spooked critter to stop."

Dee giggled. "The gods must look after ignorant girls. By all rights both of us should be six feet under by now."

"Where's your bronc?" Bryan broke in. "I'm afraid I've got a full afternoon."

Dee gave her brother an impatient glare. "He hasn't changed," she told her friend as the three of them walked toward the corral. "Can't get that man to sit still. I told him he was hyperactive, and I was going to get a doctor to prescribe tranquilizers. The only trouble is, the vet is the only one who would agree to treat him."

Bryan faked a jab in his sister's direction. "With the volume of work I give the vet, he'd probably treat me for nothing." After receiving a return jab from Dee, Bryan turned from the women and headed toward the waiting horse, boots silent in the dust.

Lynn studied his lean hips, his purposeful stride. Some people became adults before they were out of a sandbox. Maybe that's what she should have done. But her parents had let her run wild over the ranch acreage, riding and training horses, perfecting the trick riding act she preformed with Dee, competing in the barrel racing event at every rodeo she could get to. True, she had gotten a general studies degree from the local college, but even when she was caught up in the stimulation of professors and courses, she couldn't see herself sitting behind some desk in an office doing whatever it was people did when they dressed up and went inside. The only thing she'd known when she left home was that there *was* a world out there she'd barely sampled.

The two women waited outside the wooden corral as Bryan took a closer look at Red. For a few minutes they chatted about their teenage exploits, two old friends working at reestablishing the bonds of their relationship. Finally Dee took Lynn's hands. "Marc?" she asked gently. "I'm sorry things didn't work out for the two of you."

Lynn wasn't going to avoid the subject. "It was for the best," she said slowly. "Marc and I were so different. Everyone saw it except me, I guess. Maybe I was in love with love. Maybe I tried to make something out of nothing because I thought he'd put an end to the restlessness I was feeling. I wanted— Oh, I don't know what I wanted then.''

"Who does? There aren't many of us who stay on the same track all our lives.''

"But Marc wasn't on any track. That's what drove me crazy about him.'' Lynn laughed and waved her hand, swatting at the past. "Later. Give me one of your high calorie cups of hot chocolate, and get me in a mellow mood, and we can dissect the demise of my one serious romance. Not that, in retrospect, it was that serious.''

"What about the old restless spirit? What was it you told me, that you were going to see what else the world had to offer? Now you're back.''

Only Dee could be that direct. "Moving to Arizona was something I thought I had to do, all right. The appeal of glittering lights. Life in the fast lane.''

Bryan's request for a saddle brought an end to the conversation. Although Lynn offered to hold Red while Bryan saddled him, he informed her that he needed to know how difficult it was going to be to handle the animal.

"Don't argue with him,'' Dee warned in a stage whisper. "That's one stubborn cowboy. But he's right. We want a horse who'll give a cowboy his money's worth in the arena, but if he's impossible to handle when no one's on his back, he's more trouble than he's worth.''

Lynn didn't respond. Her attention was focused on the lean, hard man hefting a saddle easily onto Red's back. The picture was timeless. A hundred years ago or today the gestures would have been the same. Animal and man; strength and intelligence.

Although Bryan handled Red firmly, Lynn knew the horse would never suffer cruel treatment in this man's hands. He was simply establishing a working relationship with Red. It was important that Red learn he couldn't intimidate Bryan. It was equally important that Red realize he could expect fair and consistent treatment from the man getting ready to ride him.

"He's going to ride, isn't he?" Dee shook her head. "That dumb brother of mine still has two cracked ribs, compliments of a Brahma in Mesquite. I swear, that fool gets busted up more than the cowboys."

Lynn held her breath. Bryan was going to ride the animal despite his injured ribs.

Bryan was releasing the snubbing rope and swinging into the saddle before Lynn realized that Red wasn't wearing a bridle. She grasped Dee's arm. "He's crazy!"

"You're telling me," Dee shot back as Red gathered his legs under him.

The big animal was off, head tucked low between his front legs, each jump jarring the ground. Bryan rode with one hand on the saddle horn, the other raised high in the air. His cowboy hat flew off on the third jump, leaving his mass of thick black hair to fly about wildly. With each bucking motion, his head was thrown back; his outstretched boots still raked along Red's shoulders as required during a bucking event.

"No timing!" Lynn groaned. "There's no timing to Red's bucking."

"That's good," Dee yelled back. "He's going to throw a lot of cowboys."

But not Bryan Stone. Lynn stopped thinking about taped ribs and the strain on Bryan's pumping knees. She was thinking of nothing except the simple beauty of a well-tuned athlete putting himself against the full strength of a powerful animal. Man and horse weren't separate creatures. They functioned as a single unit—a dynamic, exciting unit.

Thirty seconds, a minute, and then Red's bucking action began to reveal the effort he was putting out. Almost imperceptibly the gelding slowed. It was then that Bryan leaned to one side and catapulted himself from the saddle. He landed on heeled boots and bolted for the fence. He was up and over before Red stopped his attack on the ground.

"Want him to think he's the winner!" Bryan gasped as Lynn and Dee joined him. Sweat coated his neck and ran down the sides of his face. "The last thing you want to do is break a bronc's spirit."

"You rode him," Lynn said. "He isn't good enough."

"He's good, all right. I have the feeling he'll always do the unexpected. He doesn't hate humans. And he certainly isn't afraid of them. He just doesn't want to be ridden." Bryan glanced over at the still bucking horse. He took a deep breath, pressed his right hand to his side and continued. "Are you ready to talk price?"

The swiftness with which Bryan made his decision caught Lynn off balance. She was still thinking about the ride, about Bryan's hand over his ribs, the set to his mouth that said he was in pain. "I don't know," she stammered. "I've never had an animal on the rodeo circuit before."

Dee squeezed her shoulder. "Be ruthless. A good saddle bronc is worth thousands."

With Dee acting as the go-between, Bryan and Lynn arrived at a price. Bryan walked to his truck and wrote out a check. "I don't think I'll change his name," he said as he handed her the check. "There's a certain punch to 'Red.'"

Lynn focused on his chiseled features. It was a face she'd known all her life, and yet something had changed. Or maybe it was she who'd changed. She was no longer just a girl admiring the raw courage of her friend's older brother. "When are you going to take Red?"

"Now. That's why I brought the horse trailer."

"Oh. Then, you were already pretty sure Red was right for you, weren't you?"

Bryan nodded. "It's the right decision, Lynn. It just should have been made earlier."

"He hasn't changed, has he," Lynn said to Dee as Bryan was backing the trailer around. "Still as abrupt as ever."

"Not really." Dee planted her hands in her back pockets. "Big brother is getting downright mellow in his old age. He always had a rapport with animals, but I think he's finally realized people are more complex than he thought they were. He's even been in love."

"Bryan's in love?"

"Past tense," Dee supplied. "It was one of those whirlwind things. Heather was beautiful. Made the local girls look like draft horses at a thoroughbred race. Bryan fell hard. And when it didn't work out—"

"Why didn't it work?"

"That, my friend, is something Bryan has never revealed. Let's just say that one day the lady in question was in the picture and the next she wasn't. As soon as he could, Bryan took off on that stallion of his, and no one saw him for three days."

"We all make mistakes when the heart is involved."

"Not me. I'm immune." Dee laughed but the sound was a little flat. "I wish I could say the same for that character." Dee nodded in the direction of her brother. "If he'd had some crushes while he was growing up, he'd have built up some immunity."

Lynn slipped the check into the back pocket of her jeans and watched Bryan head into the corral after Red. Although the horse was still blowing hard and looking wild-eyed, he allowed Bryan to slip a halter on him. Bryan spoke softly to the horse as he led him out of the corral and easily walked him into the trailer.

"How are your ribs?" Lynn asked once Red was securely in the trailer. The thought of Bryan experiencing pain upset her.

Bryan glanced at his sister as if surprised that his ribs should be a topic of conversation. "They're okay. You ready to go, Dee?"

"Brothers!" Dee snapped. "Who needs them? Lynn, you've got to come over for dinner. Tomorrow night and no arguments. We have so much to talk about. That fascinating dissection you mentioned."

"Oh, Dee, I'd love to," Lynn admitted. "But Mom's alone. I don't want to leave her."

Bryan entered the conversation. "Bring her along, then. I enjoy talking to her."

"You do?" Lynn stammered before giving herself time to think. Of course Bryan did. He'd taken time to be with her parents the day her father died—something she hadn't been able to do. "Bryan? You've been a good neighbor. I want to thank you for that."

"Didn't you think I would be? Lynn, your parents had a need. I hope I filled it."

Lynn retreated from whatever might or might not have been in Bryan's words. "You did. I just wish I'd been there."

Bryan hoisted himself into the cab of the truck. "I wish you had, too."

Shaken, Lynn stepped back to allow Bryan to turn the truck around. She stood with her hand shielding her eyes against the sun, automatically nodding in response to Dee's wave. She couldn't be sure, but she thought Bryan was watching her in the rearview mirror. His final words held her in place. Was he blaming her for not being with her parents? Even if he was, there wasn't anything she could do about it.

Lynn stared at the empty corral that had earlier held Red, trying to put together the pieces of the puzzle that was her life. There were two things she wanted to explore and they both revolved around horses. It shouldn't be hard to start her own horse training school. She'd learned enough in Phoenix to be able to train pleasure as well as working horses. And the name Walker meant something to the ranching people in Harney county.

But that was only one of the possibilities. The other, which was still more a dream than reality, would have to wait until she had more money. That dream called for a top-rate barrel racing horse and the challenge of competing professionally.

Chapter Three

When Lynn and her mother made the fifteen-mile drive to the Stone ranch the next evening, Lynn left behind her jeans. She'd had scant opportunities to wear a dress in her life and the combination of looking forward to an evening with the Stones plus a moon so clear it made her want to weep, put Lynn in a rare mood to present herself as a feminine creature.

"That moon's exquisite," Lynn said as she and her mother were getting into her car. "I wonder if a night can properly be called beautiful?"

"You look beautiful yourself," Carol replied. "You should wear a dress more often."

"It's not too practical when you're spending the day on a horse." Lynn lifted the hem of her ankle-length copper-colored skirt with buttons running from waistband to hem. Her blouse was soft white, high at the collar with layers of lace and ruffles setting off the sheen of hair softly flowing over her shoulders instead of pulled back into the practical braids she usually wore. "I feel a bit like a fairy princess with this long skirt. I just hope I don't have to jump out of the way of one of the Stone bulls."

"I imagine Bryan will make sure they stay corralled. If he doesn't take note of you in that dress, I don't think there's any hope for him."

"Bryan Stone wouldn't notice if I came wrapped in cheesecloth. He thinks of me as a carbon copy of his sister, if he thinks of me at all."

"I hope you're wrong about that." Carol looked approvingly at her daughter's light touch with eye shadow and mascara. "I know how he handles animals when they need a gentle touch. He's capable of doing the same with a woman."

"Mom!" Lynn stared at her mother in mock astonishment. "You're old enough to be his mother."

"That doesn't mean I'm blind," Carol laughed. "Us Walkers are pretty good judges of horseflesh. We can be good judges of what makes a man a man as well."

There was no arguing with her mother. Lynn smiled as she drove, the moon awakening anew her appreciation of the land around her as the clean night air drifted in the open window.

Lynn could probably drive to the Stone ranch with her eyes closed because little had changed about it. She could see new wooden fencing around the acreage closest to the county road and soon saw why. The growing stock of Brahma bulls was now being pastured there.

"They look so peaceful," Lynn observed as she drove past the great dozing creatures. These were the most feared and respected creatures on the rodeo circuit.

"You think so? Maybe you'd like to go scratch that one between the ears." Carol pointed at a bull weighing over a ton. One horn angled toward the front of his head while the other stuck straight out, a lethal weapon to be used against any cowboy who might get in its way.

Lynn shook her head. "I'll pass, thank you. I heard that one of the Stone bulls was ridden only once last year. No one stayed on him at The Finals. I wonder if he's out there. Can you imagine hauling a load of those if they all started acting up?"

"I can't understand why anyone would want to supply rodeo stock when they can make a living raising sheep," Carol observed in a continuation of what had been a long-running mock argument between the two families.

Lynn nodded in agreement, and yet she understood why Bryan Stone was a rodeo contractor. She'd seen the vitality in his eyes. A man who felt that way about life needed more of a challenge than raising sheep. Supplying bucking bulls and broncs, plus the steers and calves needed for the roping events added up to a responsible and exciting career.

The interior of the Stone main house was ablaze with lights. There were several small structures near the main house where the hired help and their families lived. Carol opened her door the minute Lynn stopped the engine, but Lynn hesitated. The ranch had a scent all its own. The mixture of irrigated pasture, hay and sage took Lynn back to the years when a girl with blond pigtails had lived for the moments when she could cling on the back of a hard-pounding quarter horse. Tonight she couldn't remember why she'd ever wanted to leave that.

"Lynn? Are you coming?" her mother prompted. "I want to see the expression on their faces when I show up with my beautiful daughter."

Lynn smiled and joined her mother. Carol Walker had always told her she was beautiful, but Lynn had never cared enough to try to determine if that was anything more than mother talk. As long as she could ride a horse, that was all she required of her body.

Dee opened the door before they reached it. "I thought you were never going to get here. You're lucky I haven't burned everything." She held Lynn at arm's length. "Jeans don't do you justice."

Lynn grimaced self-consciously. "You're wearing slacks. Am I overdressed?"

"Are you kidding? That blouse is stunning. I know you didn't get it around here. Of course you can almost see through it, but if that's what you want—"

Lynn had thought the front ruffles made up for the thin fabric, but now she wasn't so sure. With a toss of her head, she decided not to let it bother her. "I've been saving up my questions all day," Lynn teased. "How's the love life going? The last I knew you were stringing along about three men. What happened? Couldn't you make up your mind?"

Dee stopped at the entrance to the living room with its reddish-brown carpet and large masculine chairs. "That's about the size of it. Actually—" Dee turned serious "—I think my taste in men is changing. I used to wind up with characters who said 'me, me, me, me,' all the time. Now, give me someone who understands the price of hay any day. Someone who...I guess someone who makes me feel complete." Dee blinked rapidly and changed the subject. "I'm just glad we were home this week. I swear, once spring and the real rodeo season starts we're like gypsies. I mean it. I missed you so much. You know what would be wonderful? If you could go with us."

"What would I do?" Lynn asked, not understanding why the answer meant as much to her as it did.

"I don't know. Drive a truck. Load and unload stock. We had to fire a hand last week. I haven't had time to find a replacement."

"Are you serious?"

"About you being a hired hand? Of course not."

Lynn was aware of the contrast between the room and Dee. Although her friend usually wore Western attire, there was something delicate about Dee that didn't quite blend with the house's most used room. It was definitely a man's room. Bryan's room.

Carol was saying something about feeling bad because she hadn't had the Stones over lately, when a side door opened and Bryan filled the room. His boots still carried residues of dirt and his hat was pulled down over his eyes. He slipped a coil of rope off his arm and dropped it onto the carpet.

"This is not a stable!" Dee snapped as he threw his hat at a chair. "I guess I should consider myself lucky you didn't bring the calf in. How is the little orphan? She taking to her foster mamma?"

Bryan nodded but said nothing. He'd heard the truck pull into the driveway but hadn't hurried what he was doing in the barn. Still, although his hands were busy with the task of introducing a day-old calf to the milk supply that would keep it alive, his mind was playing another game. Lynn Walker would walk into the house with her braids tucked behind her ears. Her boots would make quiet thuds as she walked up the wooden steps.

The woman watching him wasn't someone he recognized, someone he could dismiss as a carbon copy

of his little sister. Bryan had absolutely no idea what
to do with that realization.

"You look nice," Bryan said softly, not moving.

"Thank you," Lynn whispered back, her thoughts
telescoping down until the room, her mother, Dee,
faded into nothing and only Bryan Stone remained.

Bryan's boots made no sound on the thick carpet as
he ate up the distance between them and turned to take
Carol's hands in his. "I'm glad you came," he was
saying.

"We saw the bulls as we were coming in." Lynn
stumbled into the only thing she could think of to say.
"You must have twice as many as you used to."

Bryan was watching her. "Actually we have a couple more than we need, but that's better than running
short. My folks came across the last one. Dad liked the
way he bucked. Mom thought the dark spots on his
rump would attract attention."

"I got a letter from your parents," Carol was saying. "Are they ever going to come home? Canada.
How I envy all the things they're doing. It sounds as
if they're having a wonderful time."

"They are. I think they're turning into gypsies."

"Come on," Dee said, grabbing Lynn's arm. "Let
them talk. You can help me in the kitchen."

With an effort Lynn turned toward her friend. She
was expected to speak. If she didn't, Dee—or Bryan—
might guess that something she couldn't pretend to
understand was taking place inside her. "You learned
to cook? Wonders never cease."

"There's a lot about me you don't know these days,
but this is what tonight is about. I have a million
things to tell you, followed by a million questions."
Dee pulled her into the large kitchen and closed the

door behind them. Then she hugged Lynn. "Thank you."

"For what?" Now that there was a door between her and Bryan, Lynn was returning to normal.

"For proving that my brother doesn't need glasses. I thought his eyes were going to pop out of his head when he saw you in that outfit. You might be the best thing to come into his life this year. I sure hope so," Dee said.

"Dee, he's known me forever."

"Yeah, but maybe it took your being away for him to really notice. That brother of mine!" Dee groaned as she lifted the lid on a stew. "I've lost count of how many girls have pranced by who would like to be noticed by him. Until Heather, all he could see were horses and cattle and acreage."

"Heather." The name rolled awkwardly off Lynn's tongue.

"Oh, yes, the one and only Heather Banks. She was part of a rodeo committee Bryan and I worked with. One of those first-time attempts that take so darn much work just to break even. Heather handled the finances for the committee. Not only was she gorgeous, but she had a lot of savvy to go with that body."

It was so hard to ask the next question. "What happened?"

"I don't know. Bryan and I are this close—" Dee held up two fingers pressed side by side "—but this was one time he fooled even me. All I know is that for a couple of months Bryan was down in California every chance he could get, and our long-distance bills went through the roof. Then—" Dee snapped her fingers "—nothing. The name Heather Banks never crossed his lips again. But Lynn, he's changed."

"How?"

"Well..." Dee paused. "You know there's always those weekend cowgirls hanging around rodeos. Sure, Bryan was aware they existed." Dee wrinkled her nose. "Most of those creatures have one thing on their minds. They don't care what Bryan is as a person, just the way he fills out his jeans."

"Dee!" Lynn took over the task of tearing lettuce for a salad. "Aren't you the one who falls in love with every hunk who comes your way? Why should you care what kind of woman Bryan is attracted to?"

"Because he's my brother, and I love him. And if you ever tell him that, I'll wring your neck. Don't get mad for what I'm going to say, okay?" Dee asked seriously. "My best friend fell in love with the wrong man. Then the same thing happened to my brother. That's a lot more serious than when we came home with notes from our teachers because we were goofing off."

"Bryan didn't get in hot water in school, remember?" Lynn pointed out. "You and I covered that department pretty well."

"True. What I'm saying is that when he fell in love, it was with a bang. And when he hurt, he hurt. I hate seeing him hurt."

So do I, Lynn said to herself without questioning where the thought came from. Dee was right. Bryan was special. Maybe it was because he was part of the spirit that turned wild prairie land into something of value. Maybe the romantic notion of the cowboy riding the range with nothing between him and death but courage, a horse and a gun still lived in Bryan Stone.

"People have to live their own lives, Dee," Lynn pointed out. "I might not have much to show for having been engaged, but I did learn that."

"Was it awful? I'm sorry. Don't answer if you don't want to."

"I don't mind." Lynn waved a finger under Dee's nose. "Dee, before you get married, ask the man what he wants out of life."

"First I have to find a man. I don't know if I'm ever going to do that. What did Marc want?" Dee took what was left of the head of lettuce from Lynn and returned it to the refrigerator.

"Beats the heck out of me."

"Didn't you talk about that kind of thing?" Dee asked in her candid way.

"I thought we did." Lynn didn't mind being probed by her friend. "When we started going together, I told Marc I was determined to experience the big, bad world. I didn't want to wind up eighty years old thinking I'd never been anything but a country hick."

"And Marc had already lived in what, at least a half dozen states." Dee shook her head. "Do you know what I thought of when you told me about him? You were the farmer's daughter and he the traveling salesman."

"That sounds about right."

Dee rattled on. "Wasn't he dabbling in computers or something?"

"Or something. Dee, you wouldn't believe the grandiose plans Marc had. He was going to open his own computer sales business. Turn it into a franchise. And I believed him. That's the really stupid thing." Lynn shook her head at the naive creature she had been back then. "I mean, what did I know about computers? I believed it when he told me he had the financial backing necessary. Do you know who the financial backer was going to be?'' Lynn tapped herself on the chest. ''Marc wanted us to save everything I made so he could get things off the ground. Only, by the time I had three thousand dollars in the bank, Marc was off on another tangent. This time it was a travel agency. At least I think it was a travel agency that came next.''

''He sounds like a flake.''

''He is a flake.'' Lynn smiled again. ''He really isn't a bad sort, Dee. He just isn't good husband material.''

''Who decided it wasn't going to work?''

Again Lynn tapped herself on the chest. ''He was living in a building that should have been condemned twenty years ago because he was too busy running around to hold down a real job. Dee, the neighbors were three feet away.'' Lynn's hand strayed to her forehead. She pressed hard, trying to push away the claustrophobic feeling that returned every time she thought about that period of her life. ''I tried to tell Marc I'd lose my mind if I had to live there.''

''I'm sorry.'' Dee had turned away from the stove and was watching Lynn closely.

''So am I.'' Lynn took a steadying breath. ''Anyway, I quit the receptionist's job I had, got that job at the barrel racing school and gave Marc back his ring. I started thinking about leaving Arizona the minute I realized I wasn't going to be taking Marc's name, but because I didn't know where I wanted to go, I stayed in Phoenix. Until Dad died.''

''You're back now,'' Dee said gently. ''That's what counts.''

"At least the next time a fast-talking man comes around promising me the world, I won't be taken in. The only thing I'm interested in these days is figuring out how I'm going to support myself."

"Won't you be staying at the ranch? I talked to Bullet after the funeral. He was so...he wasn't ready to have his father die. I think it helped him to have me to talk to. He said that having the ranch as home base has made things so much easier for him."

"Bullet's hardly ever here." Lynn lowered her voice so there was no chance of it carrying. "Chet's going to be managing the ranch. The last thing he needs is a kid sister underfoot. I want a place to call my own."

"What do you want to do?"

Lynn was grateful for the question. "I can make money training horses, but I'd also like to try the circuit. I was good once. Maybe I still am. Dee, I haven't forgotten how to ride. How it feels to compete. But that's down the road a while. I don't have the money for a horse."

The kitchen door opened and Lynn's mother and Bryan stepped it. "What are you girls talking about?" Carol Walker asked. "Dee, you haven't burned dinner have you?" Bryan stood behind Carol, arms easy at his side, coal eyes taking in everything.

"For once, no." Dee picked up the stew and started for the dining room. "Lynn was just making an observation about the attraction of rodeo life."

"One crazy man in the family is quite enough. It terrifies me to think about Bullet in the riding events," Carol said as the four were sitting down, Lynn to Bryan's right. "If I hear one word from my daughter about getting on a Stone bull, I'll lock her up and throw away the key."

"That's one thing you'll never have to worry about," Lynn reassured her mother. "Give me a well-trained quarter horse any day."

"They aren't easy to come by," Bryan pointed out. "You aren't going to find many Nevada Girls."

"I know. I just wish I had the money..." Lynn paused. Wishing didn't accomplish anything.

The conversation soon turned to other things. Lynn said little during dinner. Instead she listened as Bryan recounted stories from the years when his parents were getting the contracting business off the ground while raising two children. In a way, Lynn envied Bryan. Contracting had been a ready-made business for him to fall into and help expand as he grew up. He'd always known what he wanted out of life and had never strayed from that goal. As a teenager, Lynn had been told by rodeo old-timers that she had what it took to put her at the top of the barrel racing circuit. She'd explored it for a few years, but the need to experience more than Harney county had been strong in her then. She'd turned her back on Nevada Girl, and on the dream that was surfacing again now.

At length, Bryan pushed back his chair. "Excuse me, ladies," he said. "I'm going to take a last look at that orphan calf. His foster mother still has some reservations about taking on another youngster."

"Bryan, take Lynn with you," Carol insisted as she helped Dee collect the dishes. "She hasn't seen enough calves lately."

"You don't have—" Lynn started but Bryan's arm around her shoulders stopped her.

"You heard your mother," Bryan said softly. "It won't hurt to see another calf."

Lynn went where the strong arm steered her. And
yet, although she kept pace, she was afraid to be alone
with Bryan. Afraid he might ask where she'd been
when her father was dying. They stepped outside and
walked without speaking to the smaller of the two
barns on the Stone property. The full moon revealed
the outbuilding's silhouette but not clearly enough
that Lynn felt she could trust her footing without
Bryan's guidance.

"Your mother's glad to have you back," Bryan
said. "She's been worried about you."

"How do you know?"

"It's in her eyes every time she talks about you."

"My mother talks to you about me?"

"Sometimes," was all Bryan said.

Lynn pushed back the questions raised by that single word and concentrated on the unaccustomed feeling of loose fabric draped around her bare legs. If she
didn't, she might have lost herself in the pure emotion of a moonlit night.

The emotion was one better kept to herself. This
moment was for nothing more than seeing a newborn
calf.

The white-faced heifer was bedded down beside her
adopted mother in the stall nearest the barn's entrance. Beside the newcomer lay the cow's natural calf.
Lynn moved away from Bryan and leaned over the
stall door, her eyes soft with the knowledge that this
was one orphan who wouldn't go through life without a warm side to snuggle against.

"It doesn't take much to make an animal happy,"
she whispered. "A warm bed, enough to eat. I think
humans are the only creatures who complicate their
lives by asking for more."

"We do that, don't we?"

There didn't seem to be anything Lynn needed to say. They understood each other; that was enough. This was what Marc had never experienced. He couldn't understand this deep acceptance of the basic things in life. Lynn sighed.

"What are you thinking about?"

Lynn pulled her thoughts and eyes away from the stall and turned toward Bryan. "The past. Putting it to rest."

"You didn't like your work in Phoenix, did you." It wasn't a question.

"Not really. My boss's ideas about how to handle horses weren't the same as mine. And I'm used to being my own boss."

"I think it's more than that, Lynn. A person can't be happy when they're not where their heart needs to be." Bryan wasn't looking at her. "I used to think about that. When I was in high school it seemed like everyone else could hardly wait to move. They were all headed for L.A. or Portland, anyplace where they didn't roll up the sidewalks at night. I was the odd one because I was content with staying here. I don't question that anymore."

"Dee always said you were meant to live outside." Bryan had never opened himself up like this to her before. Lynn didn't know how to handle what was happening.

"There was never anyone to bring me inside." Bryan turned away from her. "Come on. It's time we went back."

Lynn nodded. She was both challenged and intrigued by the potential for relating to Bryan as an adult, but that would have to come in his own time, at

his own pace. Silently Lynn followed him back outside. She didn't think there could ever be anything or
anyone with the power to take this man from the life-
style he'd been born to. She wondered if Heather
Banks had tried.

When she least expected it, Bryan turned toward
her, his head bent. He reached out and placed his
hands, light and questioning, on her upper arms.
Without thinking Lynn lifted her face toward him.

"You've changed," he whispered.

"We've all changed."

Her voice was soft. Softer than he remembered.

The impulse, the desire to kiss Lynn was strong. But
then he remembered who he was, who she was.

Bryan's hands slid off Lynn. Talking about ordi-
nary things wasn't easy. "I hope I have a chance to
talk to Chet before we have to leave," he said. "I'm
thinking of having a new well drilled. He might want
one done for your place at the same time."

Bryan started back toward the house again. Lynn
followed after him, slowly. "I'll have him call you,"
she said in the same soft voice that had caught him off
guard before.

Bryan knew he didn't dare turn around.

Chapter Four

Bullet wasn't expected for at least another three hours, but Lynn was already listening for the sound of her brother's pickup. She should have had enough distraction now that Chet and his family were here, but Chet was deep in discussion with their mother, and his wife Angie was busy trying to settle the children into their new rooms.

Sighing, Lynn turned away from the window and forced herself to get started on a family dinner. She turned on the radio, needing the companionship of talk and music. She'd cut up two chickens and was working on a fruit salad when Angie came into the room. Angie poured two glasses of ice tea and handed one to Lynn before speaking.

"Those wild men of mine are so darn excited about having all this room." Angie pressed her glass against her cheek and laughed. "Be glad you're single. Kids are wonderful, but any woman who thinks she's going to survive motherhood with her sanity intact doesn't know what she's talking about." Angie took a healthy swallow of her tea. "I'm sure Chet doesn't want me to say anything, but he's nervous about taking over the ranch."

Lynn nodded in understanding. "I know my big brother. He takes things so seriously. He's going to be harder on himself than anyone else is."

"Don't I know it." Angie reached into the refrigerator for the cookie dough she'd mixed up earlier and started to roll it into balls. "That's exactly what I told him. He agrees, but that doesn't make things easier for him. He grew up here, but back then he didn't have the responsibility. He keeps saying he wishes he was as laid back as Bullet."

"Bullet, laid back?" Lynn laughed. "That's putting it mildly. I remember—" she laughed again "—he'd failed some big math test his senior year and was an inch away from flunking the course. I would have been burning the midnight oil trying to remedy the situation, but not Bullet. He was trying to scrounge the money to enter a rodeo. That, he told the folks, was a lot more important than math because he had no intention of needing math on the road. He didn't take it too kindly when Dad pointed out that at the rate he was going, he'd never have enough money to need to add it up."

"You dad said that?" Angie stopped what she was doing. "I didn't get to know William well; that bothered me. But I always thought he was a pretty serious man. I mean, he wasn't well and there was the burden of the ranch."

"He teased Bullet more than Chet or me," Lynn explained. "I think it's because, deep down, there was more of Dad in Bullet than in Chet. Dad—" Lynn paused, her mood softening at the memory. "He followed the rodeo circuit himself before the kids came along."

Angie mixed sugar and cinnamon together in a bowl and started to roll the cookie dough in the mixture. "I see the same thing happening to my crew. Chet loves all of his kids, don't get me wrong, but even though he's only six, Chad is more like his dad than Mike is. Missy's a little young to have decided on her life's mission, other than driving her mother crazy, that is."

With the radio playing Western songs, the afternoon slid away. Lynn clung to the evening's promise. Soon she would have Bullet to talk to. He'd catch her up on how the rodeo season was going, his hopes and plans. He'd ask her about what she was going to do.

Lynn lost track of what Angie was saying. What would she tell Bullet? She'd found a rental some twenty miles from the ranch, but since the little house wouldn't become available for another week, she was still living at the ranch. She'd put out feelers and figured she could make a living teaching riding skills and training horses, but she'd yet to advertise. If— No, when she did, she would be tied down.

HOURS LATER, AFTER BULLET had been welcomed back into the fold, the meal eaten and the children played with, Lynn and Bullet found their time alone. Although it was dark, brother and sister walked out to the pasture that held the ewes and their lambs. Lynn concentrated on the lean, compact man with eyes that gave out as much as she held back.

"I was so broke in Mesquite I didn't know where my next meal was coming from," Bullet said as a lamb let out a shrill bleat. "If it wasn't for a rodeo clown who took pity on me, I would have been sleeping in the cab of my truck."

"And of course you told Mom you were living high off the hog."

"Something like that."

"Something like that, nothing." Lynn rested her elbows on a wooden railing. "You didn't con Mom, you know. Why do you think your birthday check came a month early?"

Bullet looked down at his sister. Lynn lifted her eyes to meet his gaze. Although they hadn't seen each other for the better part of a year, thoughts and words flowed unchecked. "Yeah. I didn't con her, did I? I just wish I knew how she knew. I mean, when I called I made it sound as if I was living off the fat of the land. I never let on—"

"I think it goes with the territory. Mother instinct. She's doing better."

"I think you're right. Those wild men, and lady, of Chet's are going to keep her young." Bullet went back to watching the sheep. "How do you think she's handling the idea of my not being able to see her again for a couple of months?" He sighed. "I wish I had more time."

"I know," Lynn said, comfortingly. "I want to be here for her, too. But, Bullet we have to live our lives. She knows that."

"Are you?"

"Am I what?" Lynn asked although she had a feeling the conversation was finally getting around to things she needed to say. And to hear.

"Living your life."

"I'm going through the motions. I've made a few decisions, a few plans." Briefly she described her hesitancy about putting down a month's rent on a house and lining up students. "I let that happen to me in

Arizona. I got sucked into the day-to-day of earning a living. Bullet, I'm afraid.''

"Talk to me, sis." Bullet pushed against her cheek with his fist, a gentle challenge. "What are you afraid of?"

It was the better part of a minute before Lynn could form the words that needed to be said. "Maybe I'm afraid of getting back on the treadmill."

"It sounds serious."

"It is serious." Lynn rested her heavy head on her brother's shoulder. A wild man, people called her brother. But that was only because they didn't know him. "It really isn't fair. Chet knows what he wants out of life. He has his family. And you—you're crazy, but at least you're happy doing crazy things. But I . . . Oh, I don't know. I sound like I'm having a midlife crisis."

"At least you're getting it over with early. Do you know what I think?"

Lynn hadn't started talking about herself because she was hoping Bullet would help her come up with the answers she needed, but if he did, it wouldn't be the first time. "What do you think?"

"I think you need a man."

"Bullet!" Lynn jerked away. She could have pretended anger or indignation, but she doubted she would get away with either. "Is that what makes you so agreeable? You've got a woman?"

"No." Bullet's voice was low and serious. "I don't have one. Not that I have time for one right now, but—you know—our stodgy older brother's the lucky one. He has someone to care about him."

"Finding someone to care is a tall order. Besides, a man isn't going to be the answer to everything."

Bullet shifted his weight but kept up the pretense that they were out here to look at sheep. "Sis, I'm not always happy with the way things are, but for me now, that's the way it has to be. You don't have the same excuse."

"I'm not making excuses," Lynn started and then turned things around. "Why does it have to be like that for you?"

"I've only got a few years left to make my mark. I can't afford to get sidetracked."

When Lynn gave him a skeptical look, Bullet outlined what he'd mapped out. This year would be his third to make it to The Finals; he wanted to be number one before he quit. "I figure I've got about three good years left in me before age and injury takes its toll. If I'm at the top of the heap during those years, I'll have made enough money that I can pick and choose what I do after that. I can promote boots, hats, Western wear, you name it. I might start my own riding school. I've even thought about getting on a rodeo's steering committee. If I'm at the top, the options are there. I can see it now," Bullet finished expansively. "My mug on billboards and TV."

"More like your mug on wanted posters," Lynn pointed out in true sisterly fashion. "You're serious? This is what you want to do with your life?"

"It's the only thing," Bullet said softly before lightening the conversation with some outlandish suggestions about how he was going to invest the millions he planned to make.

Lynn soon stopped listening to the boast and focused on the passion. Rodeoing wasn't a childhood hobby that had gotten out of hand. From the first time he competed, it had shaped her brother's life. Although he'd set an almost overwhelming goal for himself, that goal was tempered with reality. Bullet slept, ate and breathed rodeo. Maybe he'd succeed and maybe he wouldn't, but he would give it his heart and soul.

Like Bullet, Lynn had grown up loving the competition that was part of the rodeo world. But somewhere along the line, Lynn had let that keen edge get blunted. She'd set her sights beyond the acreage of Harney county. She'd sought answers in new surroundings and distracted herself from the one activity that gave her real satisfaction.

"I KNOW IT'S CRAZY, Mom," she was telling her mother an hour later. "I mean, I don't have enough in savings to buy the kind of horse I need. I'm going to have to work for a long time before I can afford one. But I need a goal and this feels like the right one."

Carol Walker shifted in the large, worn chair and smoothed her nightgown over her knees. "You really want to compete?"

"I really want to compete. But don't worry, I'm not going to run off tomorrow. I've got to...one thing at a time."

Elsewhere in the house, Chet and Angie were checking on their sleeping children. Bullet, exhausted from weeks of competing and traveling, was snoring on the couch. "I'm not going to try to stop you," Carol whispered.

Lynn had been ready for a lot of things. Shock maybe. Disbelief maybe. But not this gentle acceptance. She had been picking at the blanket that covered the overstuffed chair. Now she dropped the fabric. "You aren't surprised?"

"Honey, I was young once. I didn't always want my life to revolve around this ranch."

Lynn had never thought about that, not really. She'd just always assumed that the peaceful isolation of Harney county and roots grown from acreage and sweat and dedication and pride had shaped her parents. But her mother must have looked at the options of life. And she had looked for the right man to share that life, and her heart with.

Lynn knew the ranch had been in her father's family for generations when Carol agreed to marry William Walker. His roots had already been planted deep and unshakable by the time he took a wife. What he had to offer was this land. "You knew you'd be spending the rest of your life here, didn't you?" Lynn asked.

Carol nodded. "Honey, I didn't marry until I was your age. I'd tasted the world. I knew I wanted what your father had to offer."

Lynn's smile reflected a sense of purpose. "And now I know what I want. But if I'm able to raise the money for a good barrel racer and if I decide to compete, how are you going to feel about it? I mean, it isn't the most conventional job. I'm too old to be chasing windmills."

Carol looked up at her daughter. "How old was Don Quixote? Besides, you aren't talking about windmills."

"Did anyone tell you what a good mother you are?"

"Someday, when you're a mother, you'll understand. Honey, you're too old for me to tell you what to do. There's only one thing I want to say. You'll be a long time settled down. If you have a dream, this is the time to follow it."

"You're good for me, Mom. I'm glad I can be honest with you."

"Did you ever think you couldn't be?"

"No. Of course not. I was just thinking—" Lynn felt better than she had in weeks, months maybe. "If both Bullet and I make it to The Finals, are you going to come watch us?"

"You get to the The Finals first, young lady. One step at a time."

AT THE SAME TIME Lynn and Carol Walker were sharing a quiet conversation, Bryan Stone stepped into the trailer he and his sister slept in when traveling. The trip to Globe, Arizona, had been long and hot. As usual, there'd been problems. Two calves had broken loose while being unloaded. The makeshift fencing the rodeo committee had contracted for hadn't been delivered until morning, which meant two of Bryan's hands had spent the first night riding herd on the Brahmas. Bryan had been up before dawn to relieve them. Then one of the two clowns scheduled to work the bull event hadn't shown up until the bulls were being loaded into the chutes. Maybe it was that on top of everything else that had Bryan wondering if dependable clowns were a thing of the past. If they were, the rodeo was in trouble.

He knew he should be getting some sleep. Dee was already curled into a ball on her bed. She might have preferred to spend the evening playing cards with the cowboys gathered in another trailer, but since coming to work for the company she'd learned to pace herself.

Bryan sat down on the side of his bed and pulled off his boots. Sleep. In theory it sounded great. In reality it might be impossible. Usually when he was unable to sleep, Bryan turned his thoughts to business matters. If nothing else, that way he could turn insomnia into a way of insuring that there wouldn't be any last-minute panic because a clown hadn't shown up and the bull riding event was in jeopardy. However, tonight he was thinking about a clear-eyed woman with flaxen hair.

Bryan tried to tell himself that it was because he hoped to be able to fulfill Carol's wish for her daughter tomorrow, but the explanation didn't wash. He knew that what kept him awake had nothing to do with business.

"Look, Lynn, I'd love to come over. For one thing, I haven't seen Bullet since the funeral, and I've missed that wild man. But we just got back last night, and I'm swamped. We've got to get the trucks serviced, and there are a million calls to make, and most important, if I don't do a wash, I'm not going to have anything left to wear. But I'm dying to have you see the pictures I took. Couldn't you break free for a couple of hours?"

"I've seen your pictures before," Lynn teased. "You're hopeless."

"I am not! At least I'm getting better. Don't you want to see what your best friend was able to accomplish with a rodeo that was going down for the third time? If I can't boast to you, who's left?"

Dee's request made sense. Lynn explained that she was going to help Angie get the children ready for a trip to town first, but she'd be over as soon as she could.

Lynn hurried her young niece through her bath and into the first outfit she could find. "I don't know when I'll be back, Mom," Lynn called on her way out the door. "I'll wrangle Dee and Bryan into feeding me lunch."

Carol Walker trailed after her daughter. "Those two," she said. "They're on the go so much this time of year. You're not going to get to see very much of them until winter."

The thought of weeks, months of not being able to see Dee—and Bryan—stripped away Lynn's upbeat mood. The Stones would be on the road earning a living, meeting new people, living the life she wanted to experience, while she, if she signed the contract for the rental, would spend the summer in Harney county.

A truck carrying calves had just arrived when Lynn pulled into the Stone driveway. Averting her face from the settling dust, she hurried past and into the house. Dee was on the phone. She shot Lynn a long-suffering look, shrugged and went back to her conversation. After pacing around the room for a minute or two, Lynn indicated that she was going to go back outside.

It was a short walk from the house to the loading ramp. Masculine shouts mingled with the startled bawling of skittish calves. Lynn climbed onto the top railing that formed the right side of the chute and watched as one calf after another slid down the chute and milled in confusion with those who had already been freed.

The scene was one she'd seen a hundred times. On the Walker ranch, the calves would have been sheep, but the result would be the same. The livestock that provided both families with their livelihood demanded and took huge chunks of time from those committed to their care.

"Dee said you were coming."

Lynn looked down. Bryan was staring up at her, one foot resting on the lowest railing, one hand gripping the wooden fence. His left hand was raised to ward off the sun. In the efforts of the morning, his shirt had become unbuttoned. "That's quite a truckload," she thought to tell him. "How many calves were in there?"

"Twenty-three. Dee said she'd talked to you this morning. I thought you'd be in with her."

"So did I," Lynn explained. "But she's on the phone. It sounded as if someone was giving her excuses about why a bill hadn't been paid. I don't think your sister was buying the story. Twenty-three calves? That seems like a lot."

"They have a way of growing up." Bryan's face was still uplifted, his pupils little more than pinpoints as the sun fought to invade them. "I have to keep replacing them."

"That makes sense. How was your trip? No major problems I hope."

For a couple of minutes Lynn was able to hold on to the threads of an everyday conversation, but when she jumped to the ground so that Bryan wouldn't have to continue standing in his awkward position, she gave up the pretense. Bryan Stone cared about inadequate fencing, a too small arena, a faltering loudspeaker system and a clown with a poor excuse for showing up late. All Lynn could think about was that Bryan and Dee had been gone just a week. It seemed longer.

She was wondering if she could tell him that when a shout alerted Bryan to the need to return to the unloading operation. Lynn watched him jog away. She was still watching him when Dee found her five minutes later.

Without preliminary, Dee slapped a packet of photographs into Lynn's hand. "Look quick. I know that blasted phone's going to ring again. What a zoo."

"Is it always like this?" Lynn glanced at the first few pictures seeing nothing that she hadn't seen at a hundred rodeos herself.

"This is quiet. Actually..." Dee laughed. "It's never quiet so I don't know what that would be like." Dee stopped Lynn's hand from flipping a picture to make sure she took time to study a close-up of a lean young cowboy with a hat so new that its brim wouldn't stay rolled up. "That's Pete. The sooner he realizes he can't ride the better. But, well..."

Lynn held the picture closer. Pete had an untested quality about him, the look of a kindergartner on his first day of school. He hadn't been born under a cowboy hat. "Did the two of you hit it off?"

"Sorta. Then we had to leave."

"Are you going to see him again?"

"Probably not. I don't know what's the matter with me these days." Dee groaned and rested her head dramatically on Lynn's shoulder. "Maybe I'm getting old. It wasn't that long ago that I could go out with someone, share a few laughs and go on to the next great evening. But now...I don't know." Dee lowered her voice. "I want something more, Lynn. I want... Oh, I don't know what I want."

"I think maybe you do," Lynn prompted.

"Maybe." Dee nodded. "I want someone who's looking for more than a good time and a few laughs. I want someone who won't be happy unless I'm the one who's with him. Just me. I want to be special to some man who's special to me. Is that so much to ask for?"

Lynn wasn't looking at Dee anymore. She absorbed her friend's words, which echoed her own emotions. "You mean what would it feel like to find a man who could understand me?" she asked Dee.

"A man who can put up with insanity and tears," Dee continued. "And not ask why I have to reach for him in the middle of the night."

Lynn turned toward Dee. The tears she felt were mirrored in Dee. Silently, the two reached for each other.

Then there were more pictures to look at, shots of the bull riding event taken from the top of one of the holding chutes, Bryan lifting his hat in acknowledgment of the crowd's applause, the barrel racing event. Lynn lingered over the pictures of lean, competent, brilliantly dressed women bending low over their mounts, flowing with the animals around a barrel, stabbing their hands skyward as they crossed the finish line.

Five minutes later, the phone call Dee had been trying to avoid came. Groaning, she acknowledged the shout from the cowboy who'd heard the phone and trotted back to the house. Lynn backed away from the loading chute while the now-empty truck pulled away, but before she had to decide what she was going to do with herself, Bryan rejoined her.

"Do you have a few minutes?" he asked in a tone at odds with the one he'd used while shouting orders.

"There's something I'd like your opinion on." A light touch on her elbow accompanied the request.

Without speaking, Lynn turned on her heels and followed Bryan as he made his way to the closest of the three Stone barns. "I've taken delivery on more than cattle this morning," he explained once they were inside the hay-scented, dimly lit barn. "I think I've found a pretty good one, but you're the expert."

Lynn frowned but didn't ask Bryan what he was talking about. A moment later she had her answer. The compactly muscled mare waiting impatiently in the box stall was an image of what Nevada Girl had been ten years ago. The bay with white stockings and a white blaze running down her nose looked to be about four years old and in magnificent condition. Lynn reached out to run her fingers down the blaze and was rewarded with a soft neigh. The mare lowered her head and butted her nose against Lynn's chest. "You're not going to try to tell me this is one of your rodeo animals," she said once she'd regained her balance. "And Dee said you had enough quarter horses to ride herd on the stock."

As if hearing his sister's name had reminded him of something, Bryan glanced around. "Actually this mare's a present. I was impressed with the way she handled herself, and when I heard she was for sale—"

"You bought her for Dee? Oh, Bryan, I know she'll be delighted." Lynn touched the mare's satiny nose. "But, Bryan, this horse is built for barrel racing. What if Dee starts competing again? Isn't that going to leave you shorthanded?"

"I've never been able to stop my sister from doing what she wants to before. What I need to know is,

have I bought flash or a horse with what it takes to be
a winner?''

Bryan had been raised around horses. He knew as
much about the creatures as she did. But he was asking her opinion and Lynn took that as a compliment.
''The only way I'd know that is if I rode her.''

''That's what I figured.'' Bryan pointed at the bridle
and saddle draped over the sides of the stall. ''How
about now?''

''You don't waste time, do you?''

''That's what I'm told. Dee's probably going to be
tied up inside for a while. If you could put the mare
through her paces...''

Five minutes later Lynn had settled herself onto the
mare's back and was entering the arena she and Dee
had set up back when they were performing. Three
rusting fifty-five-gallon steel drums stood ninety feet
apart in a triangular arrangement. First Lynn walked
the mare through the course, noting the animal's easy
acceptance of the objects she was being asked to walk
around. That done, Lynn returned to the edge of the
arena. The reins lay in her palm; the toes of her boots
were tucked lightly into the stirrups.

Lynn was no longer a teenager, but at that moment
she knew again the challenge that had made her teenage years so alive. She leaned forward, gathering herself, alerting the mare. ''You know how it's done, old
girl,'' she crooned. ''Bryan says you've done it before. Now let's see if you have the magic.''

Lynn sensed the same gathering of energy in the
animal that she was experiencing. Bryan stood to one
side of them, hat held high in the air. A rebel yell, a
quick drop of the hat and Lynn was off. The mare ran
low to the ground, focusing on the first barrel. As her

mount leaned into the barrel, Lynn's well-tuned body found the exact angle that would allow both horse and rider to maintain their balance. Lynn stole a glance at the barrel inches away. Good. Now the mare was straightening, muscles lengthening as she galloped for the second one. Once again, she didn't slow until the last split second as she passed within inches of the barrel.

"Yeah," Lynn whispered in admiration. "Yeah. Show us how it's done."

Lynn had worked with horses who took their turns too wide, who were incapable of trusting their rider's ability to flow around the barrel with them. Those horses might have been faster, flashier, but they hadn't had the instinct of this one.

If she hadn't been concentrating on flowing with the strength under her, Lynn could have reached out and touched the final barrel. Now the mare was focused on the finish line. Lynn leaned low over the steaming neck. Even without a riding crop to urge her on, the mare was in a full gallop.

"Yeah!" This time Lynn's cry cut through the prairie air. She laughed down at Bryan as she flew past him. "Yeah!" she yelled over her shoulder.

"She's wonderful, Bryan," she gasped once she'd stopped the mare and brought her back to where the rodeo contractor waited. "You've bought yourself a prize."

"I thought so."

"And you didn't really need me to pass approval on her, did you?"

"Nope."

"Then what was all this about?"

"Maybe it was about getting you on a horse again. What do you think?" Bryan asked. "Do you still want to race?"

"More than ever. But, Bryan, unless I have a horse like this one ... I'm just glad I won't have to compete with Dee when she's on her."

"Who says this is Dee's horse?"

It was several seconds before Lynn understood that it was her mother who had asked the question. Blinking, Lynn tore herself free from Bryan's gaze and focused on the woman standing a few feet away. "What's going on? Mom, I thought you were going into town with Angie."

"I lied." Carol was smiling, looking younger than she had in months. "What do you think of her?"

Something extraordinary was happening. "If I didn't know better, I'd think Nevada Girl was this mare's dam. They're so much alike. They have the same instincts."

"That's what Bryan thought." Carol was still smiling. "Tell me something, Lynn. If you had this one under you, would you wind up in the money?"

"I could take first with this mare, Mom."

"Do you like her?"

Lynn ran hot fingers over the mare's equally hot neck. "I love her."

"She's yours."

"Mom." Lynn couldn't breathe. Tears burned her eyes, but she refused to let them fall. This moment called for an emotion that went beyond tears. "You planned this? You paid for her?"

"Your father and I did, honey. Don't worry. There was enough money after we sold last year's lambs. We were—" Although Carol faltered, her smile remained. "We were waiting for the right time. For you to say this was what you wanted. And then for Bryan to find the right horse."

Now she could shed tears. "Thank you," Lynn mouthed. "Oh, Mom, thank you." Something touched her boot and Lynn glanced down to find Bryan looking up at her. He held out his hands, and she lowered herself into them.

And Bryan's arms lingered around her. She could feel his breath against her cheek. Absorb his strength.

Then she embraced her mother, trying to say what she had no words for.

Chapter Five

Lynn needed some time alone to sort out the changes all this would make in her life. She remounted and rode out along the small plateau that served as the southwest boundary of the Stone ranch. Under her was the strong young mare that held the promise of giving definition to her life. Dee had said this was where Bryan came when he needed to think. Lynn could understand that. The land was serving her as well. White Moon. Where the name came from, Lynn didn't know.

But White Moon ran as if born to it.

"White Moon. Do you like it, my beauty?" The mare's ears flicked back, giving Lynn encouragement to go on. "I need you. A lot more than you need me," she said looking up.

She could hear that someone was coming to join her in this lonely place. For an instant, Lynn resented the intrusion, but the feeling didn't last. She stopped White Moon and waited for the rider on the huge black horse to join her. It was Bryan. Even in a county filled with men who'd been raised on horseback, he stood out.

"Your mother sent me after you," Bryan said when he was close enough to make himself heard. "You left pretty fast, Lynn."

Lynn met Bryan's eyes. He wasn't judging or criticizing. "Is she worried?"

"I don't think she knows what to think." Bryan was leaning forward, running work-hardened fingers over his stallion's heated neck. "She's worried she's pushing you; that maybe finding a horse was something you wanted to do on your own."

"Oh, no." Lynn forced herself not to look at Bryan's hand. "It isn't that at all."

"Then what is it?"

"I don't know." Lynn tried to bite down the unexpected note of panic in her voice, but it was too late. "Don't mind me," she amended with an outward ease she didn't feel. "I just didn't expect this. They know me so well."

"No one can truly know another person, Lynn." Bryan sat tall and quiet in the saddle, his eyes scanning the horizon. Lynn believed that he was seeing not simply rocks and grasses and a land long without water, but his heritage and future. "Parents can love their children and give them guidance," he told her. "But they can never know everything that goes on inside those children's hearts."

How had he become so wise? Maybe she'd always misjudged him. "I'll talk to Mom. White Moon, that's what I'm going to call her. White Moon is what I need."

"Then you're ready to compete?" Bryan slid out of the saddle and hit the ground without making a sound. He reached for White Moon's reins and held her still while Lynn dismounted.

Lynn didn't immediately answer his question. "I know what Mom thinks about my running around the country the way Bullet does. I'll make concessions for her, but I'm going to compete."

Bryan nodded. He'd followed Lynn out to the plateau because her mother was concerned. Dee or one of the hired men could have done that, but Bryan had offered to go himself.

Now he wasn't sure that had been wise. Standing next to her, he was aware of her femininity. In an attempt to distract himself, Bryan turned away from her. "I come out here whenever I can," he told her. Shading his eyes, he pointed toward the horizon. "There's an antelope herd that's out there most of the summer."

"Antelope," Lynn whispered. "I'd forgotten how much I loved seeing them. I'm still rediscovering the things I missed while I was away."

Bryan turned back toward her; not looking at her hadn't helped. "What was that like? Did you enjoy it?"

"Some of it," Lynn admitted. "But, that's the past, Bryan." She ran her hand down White Moon's foreleg. "I'm ready to go forward."

Bryan saw the emotion glistening in her eyes. He should go back to scanning the horizon for the antelope he wouldn't be able to see without the aid of binoculars. But Lynn's eyes were pulling him to her. Demanding a response. "Something's wrong, Lynn. What is it?"

"I don't know. Maybe I... I think I've wanted this—to compete—for a long time now. I wish I'd known."

She was scaring him. Bryan didn't understand why that was, but he did know that he would never find the answer if he turned away now. "Don't," he cautioned her. "You can't relive the past. We all have to deal with what we are now."

He wasn't touching her, but that didn't lessen his impact on her. Lynn focused on her hands. They'd served her well over the years. They did whatever she requested of them. Today they didn't have enough to do.

"Bryan." The wind caught her voice as she said his name and swirled it around him.

Bryan reached out to touch her. Her arm felt slender under his hardened fingers, and yet he knew there was strength beneath her satin flesh. He felt Lynn's breath against his cheek—quick, shallow puffs of living air. Her arms were at her sides, and yet there was nothing calm or relaxed about her. He'd learned a lot about Lynn in the past few days. He'd always thought of Lynn Walker as a cowgirl and his sister's best friend. He was just beginning to learn something about the depth of emotion she was capable of. The way she talked about her mother revealed her compassion. Touching her sent him another message.

That message had a great deal to do with two people who were no longer children. People who needed to understand what had changed between them.

When she had first seen him riding toward her, Lynn had tried to block off the realization that they would be alone. She'd told herself she would listen to what he had to say, answer whatever questions he might ask and then they would return to their families and responsibilities. Now Lynn wasn't interested in talking or in listening to what was on his mind.

His hands were on her, not to force her to his will, but maybe because he needed to touch as much as she needed to be touched.

It was somehow totally right that their first kiss would happen here. This ageless place was home to both of them. Here she could taste his lips and soften hers. Here she could learn something about what he was capable of doing to her. But she wasn't yet ready to learn that.

She pulled away, feeling the loss in every pore. "I . . . my mother's going to worry."

"I know. Lynn?"

"What?"

What was he going to say? Bryan shook his head. "I didn't come here to—you know. That wasn't my intention."

"Oh."

She sounded hurt. Bryan didn't want to hurt her. The only thing he knew to give her was the truth. "Maybe it was. I'm not sure. Lynn, did Dee tell you about . . . I was in a relationship not too long ago."

"I know." Lynn touched his arm but only briefly. Somehow she felt softer, lighter than before. And yet she was wise enough to not read too much into their kiss. It had happened. That was all. "You don't have to tell me anything."

"I know I don't." Bryan started to leave and then stopped himself. "But maybe I want to."

"You don't—"

He stopped her. "I'd like to." He smiled. "Lynn, what I do for a living, it's a lot more than just a job."

"I understand," Lynn whispered in reply. "I grew up on a ranch, too, remember. I know the hold land has on a person."

"It's not just the land, Lynn. Being a rodeo contractor isn't a nine-to-five job," Bryan said, moving away as his stallion shifted to reach more tufts of grass.

"It takes whatever time it wants, doesn't it?"

"That's what Heather couldn't understand. She couldn't accept that."

Was that all that had been wrong between Bryan and Heather? Lynn wondered. He was committed to his work, and she had wanted more of him than he could give. "The two of you talked about that?"

"I told her the rodeo business was like being a slave. Even if I was a willing one, it wasn't something I could shove aside."

She and Bryan were no longer standing close enough that they could feel each other's presence. It was safer that way. "There aren't many women who could live with that, Bryan," she told him. "Women, people, need a certain amount from the people they care about."

"I know." Bryan once again turned toward Lynn. "But there were so many responsibilities. So many people depending on me."

"I understand."

With a wave of the hand, Bryan dismissed her comment. "And it was more than that, anyway. There were the physical risks."

Lynn didn't have to be told that danger was part of the life-style he'd taken on. Lynn's harsh laugh startled White Moon. "It goes with the territory."

"Heather didn't see it that way."

Heather be damned. But Lynn couldn't tell Bryan that. "I'm sorry."

"So am I." Bryan reached for the reins and pulled the stallion's head up. He planted a boot in the stirrup and swung himself into the saddle.

LYNN DIDN'T SEE BRYAN for two days. During those forty-eight hours, Lynn was able to make her mother understand how much White Moon meant to her. She did her telling with hugs and tears and a sharing of the sense of purpose that now filled her.

Lynn called the owner of the rental and told him she wasn't interested in the house, after all. That done, she concentrated on getting to know White Moon and letting the mare do the same with her. She accomplished that by spending every possible minute with White Moon—grooming her, walking her, and of course going through the barrel racing course with her until they were practically tracing it in their sleep.

On Wednesday night the Walkers invited Bryan and Dee over for dinner. The official reason was that Bullet and the Stones were leaving in the morning and no one knew when both families would be able to get together again. Lynn was uneasy about seeing Bryan but she couldn't put off the meeting forever. Maybe, she told herself, they'd look at each other and whatever had flowed between them the other day would no longer exist.

As soon as Bryan walked in the door, Lynn knew she'd been lying to herself. Somehow she found the courage to sit near him and ask questions about where Stone Stock was headed next. He was telling her about the long drive to Redding, California, that would begin tomorrow when Lynn's mother interrupted. "Have you thought about competing in Redding, honey?" she asked. "I know you and White Moon haven't had much time to work together yet, but I'd feel a lot better if you had friends around the first time you competed."

Lynn glanced in Bryan's direction. His fingers were splayed across his thighs. There was a fresh barbed-wire scratch running from his wrist to where his rolled-up sleeve began. Friends? "I don't know, Mom," Lynn stalled. "I'm still trying to get organized." The truth was, she hadn't had much luck finding a horse trailer she could afford, and the thought of actually putting her dreams to the test were as frightening as they were thrilling. What if she'd lost it? Her preliminary plan had been to enter a couple of local contests before testing herself at something as competitive as the Shasta County rodeo.

"Do it, kid." Dee had been sitting cross-legged on the carpet across from Bullet, arguing over which west Texas town held the best rodeo. "I'll record the moment for posterity with my camera. And if you mess up, I can always blackmail you by threatening to sell the negatives to the *Rodeo Sports News*."

Lynn shot her friend a don't-you-dare look. "You're not the one putting your reputation on the line," she informed Dee. "I don't want to jump in until I know whether I can still swim."

"You're not going to get any real competition in a local contest, Lynn."

Lynn didn't allow herself to look at Bryan. Although she owed him a reply, she was afraid she might reveal too much if she looked at him. "I don't have a trailer. How can I get White Moon to Redding?"

"Come with us."

Dee's solution was so simple. Too simple. It was more than a matter of finding room for White Moon in the stock trucks making the long trek. It was more than plunking down her entry fee and pitting herself against women who'd been competing for years. "I don't know," Lynn stalled. "Let me think about it."

"What's to think about?" Dee pressed. "You can get there for free. And you can pay us back by helping unload stock. You haven't seen the travel trailer Bryan and I haul with us when we're on the road. There'll be no trouble having you along."

Lynn didn't have to look at Bryan to know what would happen to the fragile calm she'd spent the past two days regaining if she was asked to sleep in a confined space with him. "You don't know what you're saying. I snore."

"You do not," Dee rejoined. "I've spent enough nights in your room to know that. Please. It's the only way we're going to be able to spend any time together."

"She's right, Lynn."

Three words from Bryan had more of an impact than anything Dee could have said. Even knowing she'd put her mother's mind at ease by traveling with the Stones hadn't been enough of a push. "I want to carry my own weight."

"You will. Believe me, you will." Dee nodded emphatically to reinforce her words. That settled, Dee held out her arm, silently challenging Bullet to an armwrestling contest. "You have no idea how many things there are to do. We can always use an extra hand, especially one who doesn't lose his temper and get himself fired. Now if we could only get Bullet—"

"No way." Bullet easily pinned Dee's arm to the carpet. He held her there, smiling. "You guys move slower than a gypsy camp."

Although the four spent another fifteen minutes discussing the logistics of Lynn joining the Stones, Lynn was unable to focus completely on the details. Somehow she would have to sleep in a trailer with Bryan only inches away. They might well sit together in the cab of a truck for hours.

Dinner was served on the picnic tables Chet and Bullet had set up on the lawn. After dessert, Dee asked Bullet if he'd show her the pictures that had been taken of him during last year's finals. Lynn had finished clearing one of the two picnic tables and was trying to drag it off the lawn when Bryan picked up the other end.

"Has your mom said anything about having both you and Bullet leaving at the same time?" Bryan asked once the table was tucked away against the side of the house.

"Not really. If it bothers her, she isn't letting on. But…" Lynn looked up at Bryan. She wouldn't try to erase their kiss from her mind. If it showed in her eyes, so be it. "I really don't think it does. She didn't try to stop me when I moved out."

"I know." Bryan's eyes said it all; he, too, was remembering. "But things are different for her now."

"Because Dad's dead."

Bryan nodded.

Again, Bryan had touched on something that needed to be resolved. If they were going to travel together, the air had to be cleared between them. "Thank you again."

"For what?"

"For being there that day, Bryan." Lynn hadn't wanted to whisper Bryan's name, to make it more than it was. But, some emotions were beyond her control.

"He died at home. That's the way he wanted it. Your father was a proud, independent man, Lynn. That's why I didn't try to make him go to the hospital."

Lynn just nodded.

"I couldn't do much for him, but I could protect his dignity."

Again Lynn nodded. There was no stopping the tears sliding past her lashes. "Dignity. It meant everything to my father."

"That and his family."

Bryan's simple words were Lynn's undoing. "I loved him," she whispered.

"So did I." Bryan's rough forefinger brushed away her tears. Another time Lynn would have been distracted by the gesture, but this evening she was locked into her father's memory, sharing him with the man who'd seen his last day. "He loved mornings," she told Bryan. "Summer mornings before it got hot. And he loved the early fall, watching Mom's garden ripen."

"He was a shark at an auction," Bryan added. "That's why this ranch is a success."

"But money didn't consume him. Being rich was never one of his goals."

"We talked about that, that last day—about a lot of things."

Lynn was still fighting tears, but her control was better than it had been a minute ago. She could picture Bryan and her father in the cool living room, talk sliding into silence as he father gave up the fight.

Her father had found his peace that day.

Bryan had been left alone.

Lynn blinked, focusing on Bryan. She saw him through the film left behind by her tears. This strong, competent, caring man had sat there, alone, knowing there was nothing he could do for his friend except let him die with dignity.

This was the man she'd kissed. This was the man she was going to be traveling with. How was she going to do that without risking losing herself in him?

"Thank you," Lynn whispered.

"For what?"

"For being a friend."

"A friend," Bryan whispered back. He might have said more if Dee and Bullet hadn't come around the side of the house at that moment. Dee was protesting something. Bullet, his arms folded over his chest, continued to shake his head.

"Your sister is the most stubborn woman in the world," Bullet proclaimed. "She refuses to admit she had a crush on the new principal when she was in the ninth grade."

Dee aimed a punch at Bullet's arm, which he ignored. "It wasn't him," she protested. "It was his truck. I would have given anything to drive that three-quarter ton."

"As long as Mr. Starwell was in it. You remember that, don't you Lynn? That's the first time Dee ever wore lipstick."

Before Lynn could admit that she barely remembered Mr. Starwell, let alone Dee's reaction to him, Dee made it clear that she could defend herself. "How would you know whether I wore lipstick or not? You got suspended from school more times than I did. You were never around."

Bullet shrugged off that undeniable fact. In fact it seemed to Lynn that her brother wasn't at all interested in continuing the argument. Instead he turned

Dee toward him with a gentleness Lynn had never seen before. "Those were good times, weren't they?" he asked.

"The best." Dee was looking up at him. "So carefree. So wild."

Lynn glanced over at Bryan. He, too, was watching the interplay between her brother and his sister. A moment later he jammed his hands into his back pockets and turned away. Without speaking to anyone, Bryan walked up the steps and into the house.

Lynn had no idea what to do with herself. Bullet and Dee were comparing youthful exploits. Bryan had gone inside, probably to talk to Chet and her mother. Lynn wanted to follow him, and yet at the same time she didn't.

So instead she walked over to the corral holding White Moon, to ask the mare what she thought of going to work full-time.

Chapter Six

It was three in the morning when the caravan of Stone Stock trucks and trailers pulled into the Shasta County fairgrounds. Lynn had been dozing in the cab of the truck that pulled Bryan and Dee's trailer while Dee drove. She roused when Dee backed the trailer into a level space. From where she sat, she could make out several barns, a long line of covered stables and wooden corrals. She'd been to about a hundred rodeos over the years; at night they were all the same.

"Time to get to work," Dee groaned. She stretched and arched her back. "Ah, the glamour of the rodeo world. Bullet should see this side of the operation. He doesn't know how easy he has it."

"Do you think he'd ever admit that? If there's one thing my brother insists on, it's being right."

"Does he?" Dee looked out at the night. "I guess I hadn't noticed."

Lynn stared over at her friend. "You're not going to start defending him, are you?"

Dee shook her head, but she hadn't turned from the small window. "Bullet can stand up for himself," she said softly.

Lynn had thought she understood what it took to put a rodeo together, but that was before she'd helped herd restless bucking horses into their corrals, had her foot stepped on by an agitated bull and been knocked to the ground by a frightened calf. Still, Lynn hung in with the rest of the crew for the two hours it took to secure the stock.

The roping horses being kept on the rodeo grounds were already nickering for breakfast by the time the last rig was driven to the far end of the fairgrounds. "Now what?" Lynn asked Dee. "I could kill for some sleep."

Dee glanced at her watch. "We've got maybe an hour before someone comes looking for us. Last one in the trailer gets to sleep standing up."

Lynn was leery about climbing into the trailer for fear of finding Bryan there, but the cramped trailer was empty. Dee yanked off her boots and dived for the nearest bed. "Take Bryan's. We'll set yours up this evening."

"But—" Lynn started to protest but managed to stop herself. Obviously Dee wouldn't have made that suggestion if she thought Bryan would be joining them. "Doesn't your brother need any sleep?"

"My brother lives on nerves. He'll collapse tonight, but I've learned he can't let go of the reins long enough to catch any sleep when we first light. This might look easy, but we live from crisis to crisis. Nothing can be taken for granted. No matter how long he's been at it, something always comes up that he hadn't counted on. Look, old friend, I'm delighted to have you along, but this is not the time for talk." With that Dee turned her face to the wall and went to sleep.

Lynn wasn't as successful at finding sleep. She could hear the bulls and calves bellowing a few yards away. Occasionally a horse stomped or squealed. Cowboys were talking to one another. The sun was coming up. And somewhere out there Bryan Stone was answering the thousand demands on his time.

Finally Lynn managed to doze off, but it seemed as if she'd been in bed only a few minutes before the trailer door banged. "Rise and shine, ladies. Dee, the humane society people are already here. You want to handle that?"

Dee was already sitting upright while Lynn was still trying to orient herself. With one hand, Dee grabbed her boots. The other raked through her hair. "Already? Have they said anything?"

"Nothing. But you know how closemouthed they are."

Lynn waited until Dee had stomped into her boots and was out the door before taking up floor space herself. Bryan was rifling through a drawer on the right side of the sink. He pulled out a sophisticated walkie-talkie system. "I got tired of yelling for my foreman," Bryan explained. "White Moon's fine. She's pawing the ground and ready for some exercise. How did you sleep?"

How Bryan had time to think about her sleep was beyond Lynn. She muttered something about needing to get used to the noise, but before she'd finished her sentence, the trailer door opened again and a tall, too-thin man poked his head in. "Angel's limping."

"Any idea what's wrong?" Bryan sounded more resigned than annoyed.

Randy Steller, Bryan's foreman, shook his head. "She doesn't want anyone near her. It's going to take both of us to get a close look at things."

"All right. Look, I'll see you there in about five minutes." Bryan had been distracted by his foreman's message, but now that Randy was backing out of the trailer, he turned again toward Lynn. Her hair was sleep tousled. Her blouse was slightly twisted around her slender waist, revealing the lines of her body. He should have lined up another trailer. This one was too small to hold them both.

"Who's Angel?" Lynn asked.

"One of my best bareback mares. Ugly as sin. Hates cramped spaces."

Lynn's laugh eased away nothing of Bryan's awareness of her. "And you call her Angel?"

"She loves having her nose scratched. As long as she has elbow room and no one tries to ride her, she's a pussycat. However, she does have a thing about having her feet looked at. Come to think of it, she's a pretty complicated female. Look, I'm sorry you didn't get much sleep."

"I got more than you did. Is there anything I can do to help?"

Bryan nodded thoughtfully, then said, "My horse needs exercise."

The stock area was filled with men and women engaged in caring for their mounts. Feeding and watering Bryan's stallion, Dee's big mare and White Moon took only a few minutes, but exercising each animal took more than an hour. Lynn had wondered at the wisdom of having a stallion among all these mares, but Stone Two was well trained and easy for her to handle.

She put the stallion back in his stall after a long gallop and looked around for Dee who she'd glimpsed once briefly flanked by a couple of men in boots and dress slacks. Instead she spotted Bryan trying to talk to three men at once. The slight slump to his shoulders told her that his sleepless night was catching up with him. Maybe he needed something to eat.

Lynn stepped closer to the group and listened, absorbing the look Bryan threw her way without understanding it. Bryan's foreman was asking him about the number of calves that should be moved to another holding pen. One of the other two men was the vet who'd been called in to look at Angel. The third was obviously not dressed for rodeo grounds. His dressy shoes were caked with dust. The same dust coated his slacks nearly to the knee. He was trying to wave a notepad under Bryan's nose.

"Look," Bryan sighed at the man. "I'd like to answer your questions, but I've got a lame horse to deal with, and my sister's busy. I thought you were coming this afternoon."

"My deadline's been pushed up. Look, Mr. Stone, I'm not going to be able to give the rodeo much coverage if I don't have any information."

Bryan's eyes swept over the rodeo grounds and rested on Lynn. "Ask her. She can answer any question about rodeos you throw her way." Before either Lynn or the reporter had time to open their mouths, Bryan, his foreman and the vet were moving off toward the stables.

Lynn could have marched after them and told Bryan that talking to a reporter hadn't been in her job description, but she'd seen the exhaustion in his eyes. "He's awfully busy right now," she explained, marveling at how agreeable she sounded. "I know he wants to give you an interview, but that horse he's worried about has to perform tonight if at all possible."

"I guess," the reporter muttered. He slapped at his slacks but the dust refused to budge. "What are you? His assistant?"

Because she couldn't bring herself to lie, Lynn didn't answer. She just steered the reporter to a quiet corner of the grounds and settled herself on a bale of hay. The man joined her, wincing because his thin slacks didn't protect his skin from the hay as well as Lynn's denim did. He started shooting questions at Lynn, quickly convincing her that this was the first rodeo he'd ever covered.

Lynn led him slowly but thoroughly through the rules of the various riding and roping events and then tried to explain what prompted a cowboy to climb on the back of a frenzied animal. "I wish I understood it better myself," she said while the reporter jotted down her words. "My brother competes in both the bareback and saddle events. I've asked him why he does it, and he couldn't explain. I'm not sure he knows, either."

The reporter shifted position, wincing as he did so. "Isn't he afraid of getting hurt?"

"I don't think most cowboys allow themselves to think about that. They're young, with the self-confidence that goes with being young. I think what it all boils down to is the challenge. That and being independent."

"Independent?"

Understanding the man's confusion, Lynn explained. "A cowboy is an athlete, but not the kind of athlete most people think about when they hear the word. There aren't any teams for a cowboy to be drafted onto, salaries to be negotiated, agents. You see..." Lynn's smile faded a little. She was thinking about how Bullet had needed to scratch for entry money when he first went on the circuit. He still had no idea whether there would be another penny coming his way, but his confidence had grown. He knew what his body was capable of accomplishing. He understood the competition. "Cowboys are self-employed."

"Are you saying this is their job?"

"For a lot of them," Lynn explained. "Some cowboys, especially when they're starting out, rodeo only on the weekends and hold regular jobs during the week. But if they want to make a name for themselves in rodeoing, they have to give it all they have. It's a young man's sport."

"And a young woman's." The reporter's gaze settled on Lynn, complimenting her, but not compromising their relationship.

"It depends on what the woman is concentrating on," Lynn replied. She hadn't been crazy about this assignment Bryan had given her, but the reporter had distinguished himself by acting as a professional. He might not know the sport, but he did know how to conduct an interview. She explained that if a man or woman concentrated on the bronc or bull events, there were only a limited number of years during which his or her body could handle the punishment. But those who focused on the calf and steer roping events or, like her, put everything into barrel racing could compete for years. "I guess it all boils down to commitment," Lynn finished. "Priorities. You could say the same thing about Bryan and some of the others he works with, the clowns in particular. There wouldn't even be a bull riding event if it weren't for them."

"What about your priorities, Miss Walker?" the reporter asked. "Is this, I mean going from rodeo to rodeo, what you want out of life?"

"It's a large part of what I want out of life right now." Lynn struggled to answer him as best she could. "There's a sense of accomplishment. Setting and meeting goals. Being part of a select community. The friendships among rodeo people are deep. We care about each other. Sometimes, when a cowboy is on the road for months at a time, other competitors are the only family he has."

"What about your family?" The reporter glanced at Lynn's left hand. "Are they with you?"

"Not my family," Lynn said softly. "Just my friends."

HOURS LATER Lynn was still thinking about her words. Dee was a friend, her closest friend. Bryan? She didn't know what he was, or what he might become, but "friend" didn't cover what she felt.

After completing the interview with the reporter, Lynn had taken a tour of the entire rodeo grounds. Although becoming familiar with her surroundings was something she'd always done when competing, she was now seeing things in a new light. Bryan's light. In one corral were the volatile Brahmas that drew the most attention. Protecting both animals and humans was Bryan's job. A few yards away was the corral holding bucking horses. Their slender legs, touchy nervous systems, and need for exercise and care were also Bryan's concern. To the rear of the arena, the calves and steers were pulling apart bales of hay. These skittish, half wild creatures needed constant monitoring to make sure they didn't hurt themselves or each other. That, too, came under Bryan's domain.

And then there was feed delivery, and making sure the hired help was doing their jobs, and coordinating with the volunteers putting on the rodeo, and answering questions from cowboys, and checking the safety of the chutes, equipment, the public address system, not to mention passing along words of warning to the clowns about the various bulls—there was no end to the list.

The next time she found Bryan, he was leaning against the wooden bull corral talking to a scarred, middle-aged man with hands as big as baseball mitts. Although Lynn had already bitten into the hot dog she'd just bought from a vendor, Bryan took it out of her hand. A few seconds later he swallowed the last bite. "Breakfast. Thanks. Lynn, do you remember Rusty Landers?"

Lynn tied to jog her memory, but only a fraction of her mind was left to concentrate on Bryan's question. The rest was occupied, making a commitment. For whatever time she spent with Bryan Stone, she would make sure he got something to eat on a regular basis. "I'm sorry," she had to admit. "I know you're familiar, but—"

"You're just not used to seeing me without my war paint," Rusty hinted. "Or the baggy red coveralls I usually wear. You were small enough to be able to walk under your horse the first time we met."

Lynn nodded in quiet recognition. "How long have you been clowning, Rusty?"

"Too long. Doctor says he's not going to bother sewing me up again if I lose one more battle with a bull. That's why I'm picking Bryan's brain." Rusty nodded at the corral. "Getting some pointers on which ones I don't dare turn my back on. I'm trying to break in a couple of replacements, but it's slow going. Jagger's one of those young, eager kids who drives you nuts with his energy. Tate, the one who's along this trip, has been with me a little longer. I thought he'd turn into something, but I don't know. That young buck likes a bottle more than he should."

"Sounds like a problem," Bryan observed.

"It could become one. He's real steady when he's sober. Nerves of steel. But when he's drinking . . ."

Lynn stepped back to allow Bryan and Rusty to continue their conversation, but it was obvious that the men believed in conducting their business as quickly as possible. A minute later Rusty tipped his nonexistent hat at Lynn, told her how much he used to enjoy watching her, and hobbled off.

"Good man," Bryan said softly. "Best in the business."

Lynn drew closer to Bryan. "He's hurt."

"Rusty's been hurt a long time. He has to retire, but it isn't easy for him. There's nothing else he wants to do."

Lynn read the humanity, the understanding in Bryan's voice and came closer. "Do you want another hot dog? I'll get you one."

"Maybe." Bryan was no longer looking at Rusty. Instead he had lowered his gaze to Lynn's upturned face. He had no idea what was happening. All he knew was that he was no longer thinking about the ache between his shoulder blades or his hot, tired eyes.

"Thanks for taking care of that reporter. Dee should have done that. The men from the humane society didn't stay long. They usually don't."

"She has a lot to do, too, Bryan," Lynn said.

"What she's probably doing is cowboy chasing."

"Yesterday she told me she had to go to a bank and then meet with the rodeo secretary."

"I know what she told you." Bryan's voice was edgy. He didn't want to criticize Dee in front of Lynn, but he needed sleep. A local feed store was trying to get away with shortchanging the stock. Angel might be too lame to compete tonight. And Lynn Walker was making it impossible to think about any of those things. "However, I don't know where on earth she is."

Surprised by the anger in Bryan's voice, Lynn leaned away from him. She was torn between loyalty to her friend and a nagging suspicion that Bryan was right. In the end, the old friendship won out. "Just because you haven't seen her for a while—"

"She was supposed to be working out some details with the announcer. She has the information on the stock, and if the announcer doesn't get it in time to memorize it—"

"All right!" Why was she snapping at Bryan? A moment ago she'd let him eat her hot dog and made a vow to make sure he didn't starve, and now all she was interested in was putting distance between them. "I'll tell you what," she said in a voice less firm than it had been a moment ago. "I'll look for Dee. You have enough to do."

"Maybe you can get my sister to figure that out. Why she has to run after every cowboy..." With that, Bryan stopped talking abruptly and turned away, long legs taking him toward some other pressing responsibility. Lynn watched him leave. He was exhausted. He hadn't been directing his temper at her. Lynn had to believe that.

LYNN FOUND DEE pulling a saddle off her horse. A young cowboy was holding on to the reins, making Dee laugh as she worked. The cowboy was Bullet.

"What are you doing here?" Lynn asked after giving her brother a surprised peck on the cheek. "You're supposed to be in Nevada or Texas or somewhere."

Bullet held up a hand to stop his sister's questions. "What are you, my keeper? I'm old enough to be let out of the house, you know. Okay." He smiled indulgently. "What happened was, the cowboy I planned to ride to Nevada with changed his mind. When he heard who had entered the Helldorado Rodeo, he figured he'd stand a better chance here. And that's the whole story, Sis."

Lynn continued to give a Bullet a skeptical look, not because she didn't believe her brother's story, but because teasing him might take her mind off the confrontation, if that's what it was, she'd had with Bryan. "Come on, admit it," she goaded him. "You're the one who backed down when he heard the big guns were going to be in Las Vegas. I'm going to make sure you're paired up with the rankest bronc the Stones have. You remember Red? He never had any use for you. You're going to be sorry you took the easy way out."

"Don't scare him off." Dee wrapped her arm through Bullet's. She almost, but not quite, batted her eyelashes at the cowboy. "I don't want to let him out of my sight until we've had an arm-wrestling re-match.''

"What for?" Bullet's gaze didn't leave Dee's up-turned face. "Wimps like you always lose."

The good-natured banter continued for a couple of minutes until Lynn remembered why she'd been searching for Dee. "Your brother—" she drew out the word, finding it easier to say than the man's name "—is on a tear. It's about something you're supposed to turn over to the announcer. Is he always like this before a rodeo? You'd think the whole thing would fall apart if it wasn't for him."

"The stats!" Dee slapped a hand to her forehead. "I've still got the darned stats." She glared at Bullet, but her eyes didn't continue the message started by her clenched teeth. "It's all your fault, cowboy. You made me forget."

Lynn waited until Dee had trotted off before point-ing out, in a sisterly fashion, that just because Bullet didn't have anything to do until his ride didn't mean other people were at his disposal. He shouldn't be bothering Dee when she had work to do. Bullet shrugged off her lecture. "So what have you been doing with your day?" he asked. "Other than getting in the way, that is?"

Lynn wasn't about to bite. She knew that no matter what she said, Bullet would tell her she wasn't doing anything important. "Actually," she said with a hint of mystery in her voice. "I'm on a mercy mission. In fact, this could be the most important task anyone is going to do here today."

"What?"

"I'm after another hot dog for Bryan Stone. If the man starves, the whole show might as well pack up and go home," she said and then turned away before Bullet could say anything more.

When she finally ran down the vendor, bought a Polish dog with all the fixings and then managed to locate Bryan, he was too busy to do more than grunt his gratitude. Her explanation that Dee had been located and was attending to business gained no more than an absent nod before Bryan again focused on what the vet was telling him. Lynn hung around long enough to hear that Angel would be risking permanent leg damage if she was ridden that night. Red, although Bryan would have preferred to give him more time to get used to rodeo life, would be the substitute.

Lynn left Bryan. It was already afternoon and before long, Lynn would be competing; the time to start proving herself had come.

Lynn slipped into the trailer to change into the red silken shirt and white jeans that she would be wearing for the event. Her hands trembled with tension. She was trying, unsuccessfully, to get her hair to trail down her back instead of curling around her cheeks when Bryan stepped inside the trailer.

"One hour," he told her absentmindedly. The sight of Lynn's white-gold hair flowing over her shoulders stopped whatever thoughts he'd had of catching a few minutes of sleep. Her Western-style shirt fit loosely, only hinting at her curves. The long sleeves hid all but her nervously moving fingers. The slender leather belt drew his eyes to her tiny waist. How had he been able to think of anything except her today?

"One hour what?" Lynn had gone back to trying to catch her reflection in the small mirror fastened to the wardrobe closet.

"One hour until we get the show on the road. I have to get changed."

Lynn still wasn't looking at him. He remembered her turning away from him earlier today, but he couldn't remember what they'd been arguing about. "Do you want me to leave?" she was asking.

"Not yet. It'll just take me a minute to change. There's a shower in one of the buildings you can use."

"I already have."

"Good." Bryan's thoughts wandered. She looked a little pale. He understood the anxiety she felt about facing her first ride. He should be calming her nerves not concentrating on... Watching her had stripped the exhaustion from his veins and left him feeling more alive than he'd been in a long time. "You're going to do fine."

"I hope so," she said cheerfully as she ran her hands down the sides of her jeans. Her smile faded. "I'll be glad when this ride's behind me."

Bryan nodded in understanding. His muscles still trembled with the need to rest, but right now being with Lynn, hearing her voice and watching her move, were things that couldn't be dismissed. He searched his mind for something else to say. "Thanks for the hot dog."

"Two," Lynn corrected him. "I supplied you with two hot dogs today."

"Did you?" Maybe he could manage to be free during the barrel racing event. He could hold White Moon's head for Lynn while she was waiting her turn. He would talk to her about something unrelated to the event so she would relax. But how could he do that if he couldn't even think beyond what she was doing to his senses now? "It's been a hectic day."

"For you it has. By the way, Bullet's here."

"Bullet?"

"That's where Dee was. Talking to my brother. They looked so happy to see each other."

Now Bryan remembered what their terse words had been about. At the time, his sister's lack of attention to business had irked him, but he no longer cared. What needed answering was how he was going to deal with Lynn Walker. Bryan muttered something about hoping Dee was caught up on her responsibilities, but if Lynn responded, he didn't take note of the words.

The exhaustion that had flowed from him a few minutes ago returned. Lynn had come closer and was removing his hat. "Bryan?" she whispered. "I'll be back in a half hour. Sleep."

The half hour was over too soon. He was aware of Lynn before he opened his eyes. There was a scent of rose about her, a light brush of perfume she'd used. "Bryan," she whispered. "The stands are filling."

The trailer was a blur. Her voice sounded hazy. The only thing about Bryan's world that was in focus were Lynn's eyes. She was smiling down at him, her nervousness seemingly gone. Bryan read gentle concern, confidence, and more. Thoughts of what that more could be brought him to a sitting position.

Lynn might be wearing boots and readying herself to gallop into an arena on the back of a twelve hundred pound animal, but for those few seconds Bryan could believe that neither of them had any existence beyond this trailer.

Seeking, he found her lips.

For Lynn, the moment slid to the edge of magic. Thinking about Bryan had chased away whatever nerves she'd been feeling about her upcoming ride, and left her aware of nothing but the journey begun by their first kiss and the steps that might be taken the next time they were in each other's arms.

Now they were there and Lynn's heart was singing.

It didn't last long enough. The trailer door opened and Dee squeezed in as she continued talking to someone outside. Because her head was still turned in the direction she'd come from, Bryan and Lynn separated before Dee noticed them.

"Sorry," she muttered before reaching past them for the outfit she planned to wear during the opening ceremonies. She didn't ask but Lynn read the silent questioning.

Lynn waited outside while Bryan and Dee dressed. She exchanged a smile with Rusty who now was unrecognizable again in his clown costume and face makeup. She studied a couple of barrel racers as the women rode slowly by. But her mind remained inside the trailer.

"What do you think?" Dee asked as she stepped outside. She was dressed entirely in baby blue. "Am I going to knock 'em dead?"

"You're going to have to beat them off with a stick," Lynn allowed. She made herself look at Dee and not back at the door.

Dee struck an affected pose and then laughed. "Yep. That's me. Femme fatale of the year. Lynn? What's going on with you and Bryan?"

Caught off guard, Lynn could only stutter. "Wh-where'd you get the idea something's going on?"

"I felt the electricity when I came in. Either something's happening or that trailer was hit by lightning."

"Or you haven't had enough sleep to know what's going on."

Dee gave Lynn a skeptical look. "I doubt that. How are you doing? Butterflies?"

"Earlier, but not now," Lynn admitted. "Don't ask me right before my ride, though."

"Yeah." Dee nodded in understanding. "Like Bryan says, a cowboy who doesn't get nervous is a fool. Don't worry. It'll all come back to you."

Influenced by her need to concentrate on her ride and not the distraction Bryan constituted, Lynn hurried off to ready White Moon. Because the barrel racing event was scheduled to take place before the riding events, Lynn saddled White Moon and rode her to the arena so that the mare could become accustomed to the feel of the place with thousands of people looking on.

Lynn found a relatively quiet spot not far from the holding chutes so she could watch the Grand Parade. Various dignitaries rode at the head followed by four attractive, brightly dressed young women holding flags that streamed behind them as they trotted around the arena. After them came Bryan.

There were at least fifteen people in the Grand Parade, but Lynn only had eyes for him. He'd exchanged his dirty shirt for a night-black one with tiny pearl buttons. His snow-white hat provided the perfect contrast. The rest of Bryan's costume was designed for work, not show. She didn't think he had even changed his jeans. Lynn committed to memory the line of his thighs pressed against his saddle, his straight, proud shoulders, his hands light and yet commanding on the stallion's reins. Others in the parade were waving to friends and relatives. But Bryan's gaze was sweeping over the loading chutes, ever alert for trouble.

LATER, as Lynn guided the galloping White Moon around the barrels, she felt almost part of the mare. Just before the start flag had dropped, Lynn had been aware of thousands of eyes on her, the sound of the announcer's voice, Bryan watching. But during the few seconds in the ring, when all attention centered on her, she knew nothing except the thrill of speed and balance, strength and grace, pride and accomplishment. She hadn't expected to win her first time back; as a result, she wasn't disappointed when her time was only a fraction above average. This time it was enough just to be doing what she loved.

Because she was one of the first women to race, Lynn was able to concentrate on those who came after her. A few were obviously not ready to compete, and a few outdid themselves, but the majority performed just about the way she had. Still, now Lynn could believe that one day soon she'd pull herself out of the ranks.

Lynn elected to stay mounted on White Moon, just outside the arena, once the riding events began. She would have preferred to find a perch on the wooden fencing near the chutes, but by unspoken agreement that went back to long before Lynn's time, that turf belonged to the cowboys. Still, she was able to look between the slats for a closer view of the action than most of the audience had. Occasionally Lynn caught a glimpse of Bryan as he checked on each animal before it catapulted itself, and its rider, into the arena. Red, perhaps spooked by his unfamiliar surroundings, ran instead of bucking. Still, his quick turn just before he would have hit the fence unseated his cowboy.

Lynn had seen her brother ride a hundred times. She could watch him sitting quietly astride his mount in chute number three without feeling the need to share some of the tension she knew he was feeling. Lynn understood that tension and fear was part of being a cowboy. Bullet lived with those emotions.

Dee joined her. "I've seen worse," she mused with her eyes on the third chute. "How old was he the first time he went to the Nationals?"

Lynn said he hadn't quite turned twenty-one. "I'm not so sure that was good," she continued as her brother waited for the gate to spring open. "He's had that early success to live up to every year since. It put a lot of pressure on him."

"Bullet handles pressure well."

"Yes. He does. Or if he doesn't, he doesn't talk about it much."

"Sometimes..." Dee's eyes were on the action. "He was talking to me about that today. He never used to. Come on, Bullet!" Dee yelled as bronc and rider exploded from the arena. "Yeah! You can do it."

Bullet did well in the saddle bronc event, one of only six cowboys to ride to the bell. He also stayed on the gelding he'd drawn for the bareback, but finished there out of the money.

During the more dangerous bull riding event, Lynn focused her attention on the riders, the clowns and the intense face of the rodeo contractor. At one point, the bull in chute number one climbed halfway out with a cowboy on its back and had to be shoved back down by Bryan and a couple of handlers. When the bull finally found freedom in the quickly opened gate, the cowboy was unseated before he reached the middle of the arena.

The cowboy landed on his shoulder, stunned, but before the bull could zero in on its target, Rusty, followed by another clown, sprinted into the arena to catch its attention. Rusty got there first, distracting the bull by pretending they were in a bullfight. At one point, Rusty's legs became tangled in the large red cloth. Lynn expected the other clown to draw the bull away from Rusty, but he was busy entertaining the crowd and seemed unaware of the danger to Rusty. Lynn held her breath; if Rusty didn't get untangled in time...

Somehow Bryan had gone from straddling the high chute to being in the arena. He was the one who threw open the escape gate, yelled to draw the bull's attention and then swatted it on the rump as it charged past him. Bryan glared at the other clown but said nothing to him.

The rodeo ran for over three hours by the time the ropers had completed their events, and the arena had become a mass of confusion during an insane event during which teams of cowboys caught and tried to ride a number of wild horses. By then Lynn had returned White Moon to her stall, wiped down and fed the mare, and was more than ready to have the fans turn the rodeo grounds back over to those who would be spending the night there. As she left the stable area she caught a glimpse of Bryan in an intense discussion with the young clown who'd messed up earlier.

She managed to find Dee, and the two women agreed to meet back at the trailer once Dee was free. Ten minutes later Bullet and then Dee joined Lynn.

Dee sat down on the bed and stuck out her foot indicating that Bullet was to take off her boot. "My poor instep," she moaned. "These things are killing me."

Bullet straddled Dee's leg, his back to her, and started pulling. "Then why do you wear them?"

"Vanity my dear man." Dee pushed on Bullet's back, grunting although he was the one doing the work. "A word about your ride tonight. Keep your toes pointed in more."

"Keep my toes where?" Bullet challenged. "Look, I'm lucky if I can remember where the ground is at that point. You try it."

"I would." Dee leaned forward and wrapped her arms around Bullet's waist. "Only I wouldn't want to show you up."

Lynn watched the two through lowered lashes. Bullet and Dee were so easy, so natural around each other. Why couldn't it be like that for her and Bryan?

She had her answer when Bryan came inside. She was too aware of him, too tuned in to his essence to be calm.

Bryan was showing every minute of the effort he'd put out since leaving the Stone ranch. For a moment he stood with his legs widespread, watching Bullet alternating between kneading and tickling his sister's instep. Then slowly, as if any movement was an effort, he turned toward Lynn. "Good ride." His voice echoed with exhaustion. "You did all right."

"Thank you." Bryan was obviously exhausted and Lynn wanted to be the one to take care of him. "Sit down," she offered. "You're out on your feet."

Bryan sat on the bed beside Lynn. His weight pulled her toward him and she slipped her right arm around his waist. "Lay back," she ordered. When he'd done so, she got up and pulled off his boots. Then, feeling his weight, his warmth, his trembling muscles, she guided his legs onto the bed. "Whatever it is—" she looked at his closed eyes "—it can wait until morning."

"I..." Bryan's voice trailed off. "Some of the committee members, they want to talk about tomorrow."

Dee reached under her bed and pulled out a pair of tennis shoes. She slipped into them and got to her feet. "I'll talk to them." She said, and she and Bullet were out the door before Bryan could say anything.

"I really should go," Bryan muttered, his eyes half open.

"You aren't going anywhere."

Again Bryan's eyes closed and Lynn watched him. He was asleep, or close to it. Lynn had put her arms around him when they kissed, but she hadn't touched him the way she wanted to now. Was he really as open and vulnerable as he now appeared? How would he respond if she turned thought into actions?

They weren't ready for this. This—whatever she was feeling—wasn't well formed enough yet for expression.

She was turning away when he reached for her. His hand caught her waist. "Lynn?"

"What?"

"Are you tired?"

Not tired. Oh, no, Bryan, not tired. "Yes."

"Then...there's room for you here."

A minute later Bryan's breath deepened and he was no longer aware of her or his surroundings. Lynn didn't begrudge him that. Tonight he needed sleep more than he needed her.

And she needed to stretch out next to him, place her hand over his chest and absorb his essence.

They were both asleep when, hours later, Dee returned. Bryan's sister looked over at her brother, sat down slowly and buried her head in her hands.

Chapter Seven

The next morning, Bryan was the first to waken. He was still disoriented as he half rose out of bed. The scents and sounds of early morning on the road fought to bring him back to reality. Lynn's soft presence next to him helped slide reality back into fantasy.

He couldn't remember why Lynn was sleeping—fully clothed—next to him. She opened her eyes, blinking in the same confusion. When she reached out and touched his forearm, Bryan remembered. He tried for a light tone. "Who poleaxed me last night? I don't think I've ever fallen asleep that fast."

"It all caught up with you. I'm sorry. You would have slept better if I hadn't been crowding you."

Crowding him was the last label Bryan would have put on what had taken place. Still, he understood her wish to tread carefully. He felt the same hesitancy, the same instinct that they were standing too close to the edge of a cliff and any step might be the wrong one. "We've got to work out the sleeping arrangements better. There isn't much room in here for three of us. Maybe if I got a cot and slept outside—"

"You'll do nothing of the kind," Lynn interrupted. "This is your home away from home. If anyone's going to sleep outside, it's going to be me."

Bryan wasn't yet awake enough to argue the point. Lynn had gotten to her feet and was leaning over the kitchen sink splashing water on her face. The cold water should have cooled her off, but it didn't. Lynn wanted to turn around, take a dangerous two steps and . . . Yet she couldn't do that.

This was crazy! Except for the first few weeks when her world had revolved around Marc, Lynn had never felt this need to touch, to talk, to be with another person. And if he didn't understand . . .

Lynn ducked into the miniscule bathroom. By the time she emerged, she had the trailer to herself. Nothing remained of Bryan except his scent and the imprint of his body on the bed. Lynn changed into a fresh outfit, ran a brush through her hair and stepped out to meet another hot northern California morning.

Today there was no breeze to take away the dry yet heavy air. Lynn rolled up her sleeves and went to feed and water White Moon. When she had finished she went to find the line leading to the pancake breakfast, which was run by a local fraternal group. It was filled with cowboys, hired hands, families. Lynn spotted Dee and Bullet near the end of the line and slid into place next to them. Bullet was trying to talk Dee into going with him to explore Redding, but to her credit, Dee, who looked as tired as Lynn felt, turned him down. "I've got a lot to do today, Bullet. Why don't you take your sister?" Dee suggested.

Bullet wrinkled up his nose. "What would I want to do that for?" His casual dismissal of his sister earned him a jab in the ribs from each woman. After they were served, Bullet spied a friend and sauntered off.

"You were up early," Lynn observed when the two women had found a place to sit. "I didn't hear you leave."

"I couldn't sleep. I'm not surprised you didn't hear me. You and my brother were pretty locked into each other."

"We were not," Lynn protested. "We—we were so tired last night. We crashed."

"Lynn, what the two of you do is your own business. I'm certainly the last one to give a lecture on relationships. Maybe being pushed together will work to both of your benefits."

Lynn tried to concentrate on her pancakes, but they could have been cardboard for all she knew. "What are you talking about?"

"I don't know what I'm talking about. I'm learning fast that I should never give advice on matters of the heart." Dee lifted serious eyes to Lynn. "If you and Bryan like each other, more power to you. And if you don't...I just hope you're not the one who winds up hurt this time."

"I've learned my lesson. One case of falling head over heels in a lifetime is all I'm entitled to." Lynn didn't believe a word of what she was saying. If she'd learned anything from her romance with Marc, it was that she should have her eyes wide open and her heart well in hand. But right now neither was true.

Bullet didn't ask if Lynn wanted to accompany him into Redding, and Lynn didn't bring it up. She was content to spend the day hanging around the rodeo grounds, bumping into old friends and making new ones and occasionally finding a chore to do that relieved Bryan and Dee of some responsibility. Because she was entered in the barrel racing event that day, she spent an hour working with White Moon, but it was too hot to ask the mare to exert herself.

She didn't speak to Bryan again until just before the evening's performance. He was talking to the vet assigned to the rodeo when Lynn came by to make sure there was enough water for the roping steers. Although Bryan only glanced at her, she could sense an ease in him that hadn't been there yesterday. "Angel's going to be able to perform tonight. That'll give Red more time to absorb his surroundings." He patted the vet on the shoulder. "Too bad you don't live in Harney county. I like the way you treat."

The vet smiled first at Lynn and then nodded at Bryan. "Wait until you get my bill. You'll be singing a different tune then. Look, you know where I'll be. Talking to this young lady has to be a lot more interesting than swapping medical theories with me."

The vet was gone before Lynn was ready to be left alone with Bryan. The stock contractor reached through the wooden fence to scratch Angel's nose. Lynn watched him, understanding that they'd left last night and this morning unresolved. Both of them had slept through the night, comfortable in each other's presence. But she, and maybe Bryan as well, had lost that sense of comfort as the day unfolded. She'd been left with awareness. And wanting. She couldn't tell Bryan that, but she couldn't pretend the feelings weren't there, either. If she said nothing, would they lose something precious?

"You don't look as rushed today," she started. "I'm glad."

Bryan muttered something about this particular committee being less organized than they were last year, and having to deal with a lot of snags yesterday, but Lynn listened with only half an ear. She suspected that Bryan was merely saying words, not caring whether Lynn understood. Finally he stopped concentrating on his bucking mare.

"About last night—" Lynn tried.

"I don't think we should let it happen again," he interrupted.

"Of course."

"You need your sleep."

"So do you."

"Then what are we going to do?"

Why did he have to throw the question to her? Lynn leaned against the railing, needing its strength. "I'm not going to kick you out of your trailer, Bryan."

"I'm not going to have you sleeping outside."

"Then—" Lynn laughed. "What are we going to do?" They weren't talking about something as unimportant as where either of them should be sleeping.

"I don't know, Lynn. I don't know."

There was a lot more that needed to be said, and no time to say it. Bryan had to rush off to change from rodeo contractor into a flashy dressed focus for the crowd. And Lynn needed to get her own performance outfit on, too. This time she dressed in the community shower area instead of taking a chance on bumping into Bryan in the trailer.

Tonight Lynn wasn't content to watch the events that came before hers from White Moon's back. Instead she found a perch some distance from the competing cowboys crowded around the chutes and settled on the top railing. Thousands of eyes were on each

cowboy and his mount as they came out of the chutes.
Lynn was the only one whose gaze followed every
move of the man who'd made all this possible.

Bryan remained mounted and in the arena during
most of the bronc riding events, but when the bulls
were being loaded into the chutes, he left Stone Two
in the hands of a cowboy so he could oversee the operation. Lynn marveled at the easy way he scrambled
from one chute to another, oblivious to the danger of
coming within reach of those great and deadly horns.
By the time the first group of cowboys had ridden and
fresh bulls were being loaded into the chutes, Lynn had
started to relax. Bryan might take risks, but that didn't
mean he was going to get himself killed.

Unfortunately, BlueBoy took them all by surprise.
The black-and-white speckled bull had allowed himself to be herded into the narrow confines of the
bucking chute. He did no more than bellow as the gate
slammed into place behind him. It wasn't until Bryan
leaned over him to slip the flank strap into place that
BlueBoy let out a squeal that could be heard above
every other sound in the arena.

BlueBoy did more than throw his head or pound the
bars with his front hooves. Screaming his opinion of
man's insane games, he threw his body skyward. In
the process, he managed to hook his front legs over the
fence, allowing him to climb halfway out of the chute.
The cowboy who'd been straddling him became an
unfortunate victim and was smashed against the bars.
Bryan was that cowboy.

Bryan's right leg was pinned between BlueBoy and
cold steel; and there wasn't a thing he could do until
the bull decided to move. Around him, other cowboys were slapping their hats in BlueBoy's face trying

to dislodge him. For five or six seconds Bryan waited silently, in pain, while activity swirled around him. Finally, with a frustrated snort, BlueBoy dropped back to the ground. The spectators, who hadn't seen Bryan's leg, applauded this unexpected excitement.

Lynn hated the sound. For a moment she hated the way Bryan earned his living. If it had been in her power, she would have rushed into the arena and begged him to do something, anything, else.

Still, no matter how great her need to push herself close to Bryan and demand proof that he hadn't been crippled, she forced herself to remain where she was. From the earliest days of rodeoing, a code of manhood had taken hold. A cowboy might be gored, knocked unconscious, or dragged around an arena. Clowns and other cowboys could and did come to his aid. But the woman in that cowboy's life, if she understood her man's need for self-respect, waited.

Lynn saw Bryan move, saw the other cowboys first surround him and then pat him on the back. She took that as the affirmation she needed. He was okay. He wasn't crippled. Lynn would have to wait until Bryan was ready to tell her how badly he'd been injured.

Although she tried to distract herself by concentrating on the rest of the bull riding event, Lynn's thoughts remained with Bryan. Occasionally she risked a look his way. He'd gone back to his responsibilities, seemingly none the worst for wear. And yet, because Lynn was tuned into Bryan, she saw the tight lines around his mouth, his slowed movements.

Just before it was time for Lynn's ride, Bryan came out to watch. She was getting better. With each ride, the quality of her performance improved. Bryan concentrated not on White Moon but on the strong, lean figure pushing the mare. He'd been right. There was a flow between horse and rider. Lynn was a natural.

She's come home, Bryan thought as White Moon whipped around the first barrel. She's where she needs to be, he admitted once the barrels were behind them and horse and rider were streaking toward the finish line. Bryan lifted his hat to her in admiration. Someday, he believed, her talent and determination would take her to the top. When that happened, she would become as single-minded as her brother. He didn't resent that. Because this was his world, he understood. But soon there wouldn't be time or room in her life for him.

When the last steer had been roped, the last calf thrown to the ground and tied, Lynn approached Bryan slowly, not wanting him to know what the waiting had cost her. He was talking intently to some of the cowboys hanging around the chutes, but when he spotted her, Bryan left his domain and joined her.

Around them calves were being herded back to their corral, spectators filed out of the stands, cowboys collected their belongings. And one of them stooped to pick up something Bryan had pointed out in the dust at the bottom of the chute.

"Are you all right?" Lynn asked.

"Fine. I'm fine. It's not the first time that's happened."

"I know." Lynn was running her hands over her thighs. She didn't drop her eyes from his. "I just—I hate seeing you hurt, Bryan."

Bryan didn't want to hear that. "You had a good ride," he told her. "You and White Moon are smooth." They were standing a few feet apart, each of them in their cowboy boots, hats obscuring their faces.

"I should have worked White Moon harder. She handles the heat better than I thought she would." Lynn was glad to see that Bryan wasn't favoring his leg.

"You have the instinct, Lynn. It'll come back to you." Bryan didn't want to rehash the accident, particularly in light of what the men had said about BlueBoy. None of the things that usually controlled his thoughts interested Bryan tonight. The last thing he wanted to think about was the question raised by a couple of the bull handlers who said that BlueBoy had acted out of character tonight; he'd reacted like an animal in pain.

Bryan had spent the day trying to avoid Lynn, trying to tell himself there shouldn't be any significance attached to their having spent the night together. But he couldn't shut off the memory of taking her in his arms. And Bryan didn't know what to do about it.

What he did know was, it would take a great deal more than exhaustion to allow him to get as close to Lynn again as he had last night without taking steps he'd never be able to retract. "I think I've got it figured out," he heard himself say. "I'm going to sleep in my foreman's trailer. Randy has room."

He didn't want to spend any more nights with her. Good, Lynn tried to tell herself as she wiped suddenly cold hands down her thighs. He'd made a wise decision. One she should be grateful for.

But Lynn remembered falling asleep with his warm, strong body next to hers. "He won't mind?" she asked.

"We've already talked about it. Randy's between girlfriends these days. He could use the company. You and Dee need more room to spread out." A mounted cowboy rode past, but Bryan wasn't distracted. To hell with his foreman's offer and with his sister's claim on the trailer. He wanted to lift Lynn in his arms, carry her to the trailer, step inside and shut out the world. She would be like silk under his hands. His mouth, made hard by the protest from his bruised leg, would soften and move until Lynn Walker knew nothing except him.

What was he thinking of? There were still a half dozen mounted cowboys in the arena. One of them was nearby, waiting for Bryan to collect his stallion. Lynn was magic—fluid magic—but it was only an illusion. She couldn't possibly be wanting what he was wanting, needing nothing more out of life than for them to be alone.

"I'll see you soon," Bryan said as he swung into his saddle. Sharp pain in his leg distracted him momentarily, but when his thoughts cleared, he realized that she hadn't moved and was looking up at him, her lips parted.

"Soon," Lynn said. Then she headed toward one of the several gates leading out of the corral. Her narrow boots kicked up small, silent puffs of dust.

Although she would rather have been alone, Lynn allowed herself to be pulled along as Dee and Bullet went in search of relaxation. "Has Bryan said anything?" Bullet asked as they prowled the grounds. "About this mishap of his? I rode BlueBoy once. Reminded me of why I don't generally go in for the bull event. But he's usually a pussycat in the chute."

Dee had taken Bullet's hand. "When did you ride BlueBoy? I don't remember that."

"What do you do? Keep track of every animal I ride?"

"Of course not." Dee was looking at the ground. "You're hardly that important. It's BlueBoy I keep track of."

A few minutes later Lynn was sitting cross-legged on the grass near a horse trailer trying to make sense out of the poker hand she'd been dealt. Poker bored her.

Still, Lynn stayed until her legs fell asleep and a half-drunk cowboy near her started making suggestions she couldn't ignore anymore. Then she wandered slowly through campers and horse trailers watching those who were due at another rodeo tomorrow and were getting ready to leave.

The suicide circuit, they called it. Lynn watched a gimpy cowboy load his roping horse into a battered trailer. He was bigger than Bullet and his bronc riding friends. He was older, permanently tanned. Lynn guessed that he had a wife and children somewhere, bills to pay. His neighbors probably wondered when he was going to settle down and find a real job like everyone else. But, because he was a roper, his rodeoing career could stretch out for several more years.

Unless he could no longer handle nights away from his family. Feeling a little sorry for him, Lynn waved at the man.

She was still trying to shake off her melancholy mood when she reached the Stone trailer. Lynn gathered her nightshirt and robe and then took a lukewarm shower in the community stalls. She was the only one there. The other cowgirls were probably all still out celebrating.

Stop it, Lynn warned herself once she was back inside the trailer. Feeling as if she'd been cast adrift wasn't going to do her any good. Lynn turned on one of the lights and tried to concentrate on the local paper she'd found in the dressing room. A few minutes later the hot, still night got to her and she shed her lightweight robe. Her nightshirt was strictly utilitarian, a soft cotton that covered her thighs but stopped short of the knees. The V neckline only hinted at what was being covered. Lynn pulled at the neckline and fanned with the newspaper, cooling herself.

Someone was outside. Lynn heard the door handle turn and glanced up. There wasn't time to ask herself whether it would be Dee or her brother before Bryan was inside. He stopped with his hand still on the knob. Lynn guessed that he hadn't expected anyone to be there. "I thought you'd— There's a lot going on out there."

"I know." The newspaper dropped from Lynn's fingers. "Have you talked to your foreman? I mean, if you need—"

"No problem." Bryan let the door close softly and took a slow step. He paused, hand poised over his right thigh.

Lynn pointed. "You did hurt yourself, didn't you?"

"It's not bad."

"I'm sure it isn't." Lynn chuckled softly. "Do you have any idea how many times I've heard Bullet say that? He'd crawl home looking like he ran into a wall and try to tell us he was just fine. What did that bull do to you?"

Bryan shrugged but didn't try to sidestep the question. "A bruise." His smile matched Lynn's. "A grandaddy of a bruise."

"That's what I thought. It's starting to stiffen up on you, isn't it?"

"A little."

Lynn rolled her eyes skyward. "Just like Bullet," she observed. "If your leg fell off, would that be a fair to middling injury? Come on." She indicated his bed. "Sit down. Let's take a look at this. You're long overdue for an ice pack."

Bryan obeyed Lynn's orders but didn't respond to her concerned look.

Lynn, however, was ready to face what had to be faced. "Take off your jeans," she told him.

"What?" Bryan clamped his hand over his thigh and winced. "I know what it looks like."

"I'm sure you do. That's what Bullet said the time he drove a sliver into his knee. Damn fool thought that was nothing, too. Off with your jeans."

Bryan hesitated for only a moment. He didn't want to appear vulnerable in front of Lynn. But Bryan had been to enough emergency rooms and prodded by enough doctors that he knew when modesty had no place. "I don't think you're going to like what you'll see," he warned her before sliding the jeans off his hips.

Lynn focused on Bryan's thigh. To look elsewhere would distract her from what, at this minute, was the only important thing. "Hmm." She leaned forward, reaching out toward the swollen, dark purple bruise. "I've seen worse. I've also seen better."

Bryan brushed Lynn's hand away. He looked down and frowned. "You aren't going to faint, are you?"

"Why should I faint?" Lynn risked a glance at Bryan's eyes and understood. He was a man of pride, with certain standards and a certain understanding of what he was. If she wasn't careful, she might jeopardize that. Lynn got up and reached for the tiny refrigerator to the left of the sink. As she suspected, the freezer compartment contained an ice pack. She handed it to him. "I thought about becoming a vet once."

"Why didn't you?"

Bryan had covered his swollen thigh with the ice pack. Already Lynn could sense some of the tightness going out of him. "Do you know how long I'd have to stay in school to become a vet?" she said teasingly. "I'd much rather bum around the country getting rich entering barrel racing events."

Bryan grunted.

"Do you think you should have that looked at?" Lynn asked him. "There might be a muscle tear." She climbed on Dee's bed and tucked her legs under her. She thought about tugging on the hem of her night-shirt but that would only call attention to the length of leg exposed.

Bryan shook his head. When she least expected it, he smiled. "If there's one thing I've learned, it's how to judge when I'm hurt and when I'm not."

"You're hurt," Lynn tried to point out. She didn't want to spend their time together discussing his injuries, but it was better, and easier, than silence.

"This?" Bryan dismissed his thigh with a shrug. As quickly as it had come, his smile left. "I've only been really hurt once, Lynn."

Her name rolling gently from his lips drew Lynn's thoughts. "When?" she asked.

Bryan didn't answer her immediately. He was staring at her, his thoughts a mystery. "I was gored once," he went on. "Did Dee tell you?"

Lynn waited for horror to fill her, but the emotion didn't come. She couldn't help thinking of scars, a panicked ride to the hospital, Bryan's pain. But his eyes were asking her to look beyond that; he needed her to accept what couldn't be changed. "No," she whispered. "Where were you?"

So Bryan told her. They'd been in Pendleton, Oregon, two years ago when a sudden lightning storm panicked the stock. The rodeo was already underway, which meant Bryan and the others were hard-pressed to herd the animals into safe enclosures before they could injure themselves. The horses, steers and calves bent to the will of their two-footed masters, but the Brahmas were a different story. Angered more than frightened, two bulls broke free. They charged into the arena, and one of them promptly raced from one end of the ring to the other, smashing his horns against the far fence. The spectators, who a few minutes before had been marveling at the wild strength of the creatures, were suddenly concerned for their safety.

That's when Bryan made his mistake. He rode into the arena with the intention of lassoing the Brahmas one at a time and forcing them into a more confined space. Because he was concentrating on the wilder of the bulls and trying to protect his stallion, Bryan failed to see the other bull start to charge. At the last instant, Bryan heard it closing in on him and gave Stone Two his head. The frightened horse spun wildly and Bryan was unseated. The bull was on him almost before he hit the ground.

Despite the light near Lynn, Bryan's face was in shadow. She sensed him drawing into himself. She could hear him breathing. "I was in the hospital for three weeks."

"What happened, Bryan?"

"Everything." Bryan poked absently at his side. "I don't remember the first week. They wanted to keep me longer but . . ."

"But you had to get out of there," Lynn prompted after he had fallen silent. She wanted to touch him, but that would have to wait. First Bryan needed to finish.

"I had too much time to think."

"About what?" Lynn hated having to ask the question, but she sensed that Bryan wouldn't be free of whatever was inside him until he'd answered her.

"About—" Bryan lifted the ice pack, poked the purple flesh with a callused finger and clamped the ice pack over it again. "Being crippled. Dying."

So that's what it was. He'd come face-to-face with his own mortality and been shaken by what he'd seen. The characters John Wayne had played might never have admitted fear, but that was a freedom not given to thinking, breathing humans. Lynn didn't try to stop her impulse. She slid forward on Dee's bed, reached out and covered Bryan's hand with her own. She waited for his eyes to meet hers, hoping she had enough understanding in her to sustain him.

But when he looked at her, Lynn was no longer thinking about a man trapped in a hospital bed wondering whether he'd ever get out of it. Instead she was seeing someone she'd once thought impenetrable who turned out to be human, after all. Someone who was strong enough to let her see that side of him.

"You made it," she said around the emotions that threatened to suck her in. "It turned out all right."

"I know." Bryan turned his hand around so that their fingers were now entwined. His eyes never left hers.

"Accidents happen." Lynn couldn't remember when or if she and Bryan had ever felt this close before. His fingers were awakening emotions deep inside her. "You—you can't go through life insulating yourself from the unexpected. That isn't your way."

"I know that, Lynn. But . . ." Bryan lifted Lynn's hand to his mouth and gently brushed his lips over her knuckles. "I felt out of control in the hospital. I had no say in what was happening to me. For a while I wanted someone else to make the decisions. Lynn, that wasn't me. I didn't recognize the man in that hospital bed."

"It was a fluke," she tried to assure him. "It's not going to happen again. You used up a lifetime of bad luck with that one round. Bryan . . ." He'd touched his lips to her knuckles again. That made it hard for her to go on. But Lynn tried again. "You lead with your head. That's the way you live your life." She looked down at her hand. It was lost in his larger one. She was lost with it. "I'm the one who leads with her heart."

Bryan concentrated on Lynn's mouth. Her lips were slightly parted, rose colored. She looked a step away from crying—or something else. "Is that wrong?" he asked her.

"It hasn't served me in very good stead. Bryan—" she tapped her chest with her free hand "—look where it's gotten me."

"What's wrong with where you are now?"

He was asking difficult questions. Impossible questions. But Lynn needed to be equal to the challenge. "Where am I?" she asked bitterly. She was thinking about her hand and the warmth that encompassed much more than her fingers. It was dangerous for them to stay here. It was impossible to leave. "I've got

the clothes on my back, a savings account that's mine
in name only. White Moon's my only real asset, and
she was a gift. I'm no further along than I was five
years ago."

"Yes, you are." Bryan whispered the words. "You
have a talent not many women do. Your goal, it's
within your reach. And you're five years wiser than
you were then."

Bryan was right. Lynn couldn't think how to go on.
Still, Bryan's eyes were asking her to continue. To
confirm or deny what he'd said. "I appreciate your
saying that, Bryan," she told him. "I needed to hear
that. Yes, I guess I can do one thing well. I can ride a
horse. But, I'll try to explain what I'm thinking.
You're logical, practical. When you do things, it's because you're looking at a goal. I follow my heart.
They're two very different things."

"Maybe." Bryan caressed the back of Lynn's hand.
"Probably. But I do have a heart. I learned that the
hard way."

Lynn forced herself to ask the question. "With
Heather?"

"With Heather." He sighed, and released Lynn's
hand.

Lynn let her now-free hand rest quietly in her lap.
Because her flesh still carried his imprint, she was able
to cope with the loss. "You make it sound like a mistake. I don't think falling in love can ever be a total
mistake."

"You don't?" Bryan's features clouded. "Lynn,
neither of us has anything to show for having been in
love."

"Don't we?" Lynn countered. "If we're talking
about material benefits then, no, I don't have any-

thing to show for my time with Marc. But that's only the surface. I now know a great deal more than I did about what it takes for a man to be good husband material, and what I need to make me happy." Outside someone laughed. Other loud voices joined in. Still, Lynn wasn't distracted. "Give yourself time, Bryan." She could have stopped there, but Lynn was a brave woman. "You'll love again."

When Bryan didn't say anything, Lynn continued. "You're a success because you've let your head rule you. I believe—" His eyes were boring into her, reaching for her deepest emotions. "I believe you have the capacity to be guided by your heart again. Just because your most intense emotions have been wrapped up in what you do for a living, doesn't mean that's the only way you'll ever live your life."

"You believe that?" Bryan wasn't blinking. There was no way she could break the intensity of his gaze. "You think I've poured everything into my work?"

"To a great extent. I'm talking about responsibility. You've carried that weight all your life."

"It's more than a sense of responsibility," he told her. "Lynn. Yes, I feel responsible for the cowboys, the fans, the rodeo committees, the animals. But it's also a commitment I've made to myself."

Was Bryan trying to tell her that Stone Stock was and would always be his first concern? Did he feel she needed to understand that about him? Lynn didn't want to hear that. She'd seen glimpses of compassion and caring, felt the constant hum of sensuality between them.

"What's wrong?"

"Nothing. Everything." Lynn thought about standing and leaving Bryan alone with his commitment. But if she moved, he would know how deeply he had affected her. "Don't mind me," she tried to speak lightly. "I envy you. I really do. At least you know what you want out of life."

Lynn was so wrong about both of them. He'd seen her ride. He knew how bright her star could shine in a barrel racing world. And Bryan couldn't believe he hadn't given himself away. Stone Stock might give his days purpose and financial security, but he wanted to share that purpose and security and he'd had too many lonely nights.

But all Bryan could see was how close she was to realizing dreams that might not leave time for him. "It's been a long day, Lynn. We're both tired. We shouldn't be trying to solve the world's problems."

Lynn slid further forward, lessening what little space was left between them. "We weren't trying to straighten out the world, Bryan. Just ourselves."

"And that's not something that can be done in one night."

"You're right." Lynn wanted to sigh, to give him some sign that she was ready to put her long day behind her, but what she felt wasn't the need for sleep. Bryan straightened, drawing Lynn's gaze and her thoughts.

But when Bryan had spoken of commitment and responsibility, he hadn't been talking about them. So Lynn stood, leaned forward and touched her mouth to his. "You're a wise man, Bryan. A beautiful, wise man."

"Because I said we can't solve the world's problems tonight?" Bryan hadn't drawn away. But she could tell he had been startled by their brief kiss. Still, he'd recovered in time to enjoy it as much as she had.

"That's part of it." She kissed him again. "You make me take my emotions out of mothballs and examine them. I'm grateful to you for that."

Bryan hated it when men made crude advances toward women. Because of the transient nature of a cowboy's life, he understood the longing to take warmth and comfort where a man could find it. Still, Bryan had always believed that one-night stands would leave him with less than he'd begun with.

When he reached for Lynn and drew her down beside him, he knew that whatever happened, or didn't happen, would never be a one-night stand. He knew too much about Lynn. She understood so much about him.

"We can still talk," he whispered once she was seated beside him. Their naked thighs were touching. He felt her warmth. She took a steadying breath.

Lynn reached for him. "We can, can't we?"

And more, Bryan thought. We can do more than talk. Her kiss a few moments ago had been a butterfly-light whisper. The one he gave her now sealed their thoughts and words and emotions.

A moment ago the rodeo grounds had been filled with the distracting sounds of men and animals. Bryan no longer heard them. The only sound that reached him was that of Lynn's quick, shallow breathing.

He didn't feel his bruise or the lingering cold from the ice pack. He had put aside his memory of the broken cattle prod that he'd found in the dust of the chute. There was only one reality. Lynn was answering his kiss.

Chapter Eight

Stone Stock supplied the Last Stand Rodeo in Coulee City, Washington, at the end of May. Two days later they were back in California for the Elks Rodeo and Parade in Santa Maria. Because there was a short break before the stock had to be in Union, Oregon, the Stones and Lynn returned home. While Bryan and Dee utilized their time to oversee repairs on the trucks, Lynn visited her family. Carol was delighted to hear that Lynn had taken third place in Santa Maria but concerned because the last time she'd heard from Bullet, he was on his way to Texas, sharing the driving with someone he'd just met. "That child's going to be the death of me yet," Carol muttered. "Will you tell me why I'm running into one son every time I turn around, and I don't even know what state the other is in?"

Lynn focused on the first part of her mother's question. "Does it feel as if Chet is underfoot?" she asked. "Having three generations and two women under one roof calls for adjustments."

To her relief, Carol waved off Lynn's concern. "It's not like that at all, honey," her mother reassured her. "This ranch is so big and there's so much for Chet to do that I don't see him until supper. The same's true for Angie. She gets the kids dressed and fed, and then she's out there working side by side with Chet. That woman loves ranching as much as the rest of us. And those grandchildren of mine..." Carol's face softened. "I'd hate to have back the quiet your dad and I had."

Lynn spent the night at the ranch, which gave her the opportunity to watch the extended family in action. She was particularly impressed with Chet's knowledge. He had already installed a computer designed to keep him up-to-date on stock and feed prices, inventory control, and what fields needed watering when. He showed Lynn how the computer allowed them to keep the ranch books up-to-date and talked about linking them to other sheep ranchers. "It's big business these days, sis," Chet explained. "I can just see Dad shaking his head at all this nonsense. Sometimes—" Chet lowered his voice. "Sometimes I get the feeling he's still here, looking over my shoulder, making sure I do it right."

"Maybe he is," Lynn agreed.

THE NEXT MORNING Lynn said a reluctant farewell and rejoined the Stones. There was barely time for her to do more than nod at Bryan and Dee before the caravan took off again. This time their destination was tiny Union, Oregon, in the northeastern part of the state. When they arrived, Lynn was convinced that the entire town had stepped in to assure that the rodeo would be a success. For a few days, the sleepy ranching community was being transformed into a wild celebration.

A little too much celebration caught up with a couple of the hands and Rusty's apprentice clowns. Although the two hands had tended to business until they had finished the job of unloading stock, they weren't around when it was time for the night feeding. Bryan and Rusty found them and Jagger and Tate at the one watering hole in town. The two hands, seeing their glaring boss come in the door, beat a hasty retreat. An embarrassed Jagger promised Rusty that he'd never again drink before a night of work. Tate, however, had already had too many beers.

"I don't care what you do," Bryan said once he and Rusty had the young clown outside. "Sleep it off. Drink half the coffee in the world. Just don't show up in the ring until you're sober."

"You ain't my boss," Tate slurred.

"No. I'm not. Look Tate, I don't want anything happening to you. Or to any of the cowboys because you're not one hundred percent sharp."

Rusty backed Bryan up. "This isn't the first time, Tate. Don't blow your career because you can't handle the bottle."

"Career? This ain't no career. This is . . ." Tate's words trailed off.

"Maybe it isn't to you," Bryan said, as he and Rusty steered Tate back toward the rodeo grounds. "But it is to us. Wait until you get a little older, with a little more at stake. Then you'll see it in another light."

"I don't know if he will," Rusty muttered. "All that talent may be going up in smoke. What am I going to do, Bryan? I can't just give up on him."

"I know you can't," Bryan sympathized. "But I can't have him around my stock in this condition. I'm sorry if he isn't going to make any money tonight, but that's the way it has to be." Bryan groaned. "How'd we get roped into riding herd on men as well as animals?"

"Beats me. Beats me."

SINCE THAT MAGICAL TIME in Bryan's trailer, Lynn had lived on the edge. She had no explanation for how a gentle awareness of each other had exploded into flames with just a kiss. Until she understood that, Lynn felt safer staying out of Bryan's path. Maybe he felt the same way. Probably, Lynn amended. Weren't his casual conversations, his rigid body, his nights spent in his foreman's trailer, proof?

As a result of having competed in several rodeos now, Lynn was able to get through the day without having her stomach tie itself in knots. Her confidence was back. When she settled in her saddle, she had only one goal. This time she was going to do better than she had the time before. She was meeting her goals and feeling good about that part of her life. In addition, Lynn went about the responsibilities she'd given herself as part of the Stone team as if born to those chores. Maybe she didn't dare get close to Bryan; maybe he didn't want her too close. But she could still carry her own weight, and feel pride in a job well done.

Lynn had thrown a rope around a bucking mare's month old foal and was checking the fit of the filly's halter the day after they arrived in Union when she noticed that a trio of grim-faced men had drawn the attention of the Stone Stock handlers. Lynn completed the necessary adjustments and freed the filly to run back to her mother. Then she walked over to the driver who drove the largest stock truck.

"Who are they?" she asked. "Don't they ever smile?"

"The A.H.A. smile?"

"The animal humane people?" Lynn frowned. "What are they doing here?"

The truck driver glanced at Lynn before snorting. "Poking around. You never know when they're going to show up."

"But out here?" Lynn questioned. "We've had them at the bigger rodeos, but—"

"That's the way they operate. I guess they figure we'll try to get away with things here that we wouldn't try in Calgary or Pendleton. Sometimes they do this because they don't have anything better to do and sometimes because someone puts a burr under their saddles."

"What kind of a burr?"

"Who knows? Some little old lady sees the sweat on a horse's back after it has carried a saddle all day and decides the creature's been overworked. Once we had a couple of young ladies call the A.H.A. because they tried to hit on Bryan and he didn't bite. All kinds of things."

"That really happened?"

"'Fraid so. Fortunately, Bryan keeps his nose clean. They didn't find anything then. They won't find anything today. Don't let it get to you, Lynn. They're just doing their job."

Just the same, Lynn was angry. She took it as a personal affront that the officials would question any treatment of Stone animals. She'd seen Bryan dismiss his own needs because a horse went lame or a couple of bulls did battle with each other. Hadn't Bryan found room for the useless filly to travel with her mother rather than separate the two? "Why don't they ask us?" Lynn demanded. "I'd love to tell them a thing or two."

The driver shrugged. "Let them poke around all they want. You and I both know they won't find any violations."

The driver was right. Although the three men remained around the rodeo grounds for several hours taking pictures, checking feed and closely examining several animals, they left before the rodeo began. Until her ride was over, she was able to dismiss the humane association officials from her mind, but now, having taken second place, she was sitting on her usual perch so she could watch Bryan at work.

This was what the officials should have seen, Lynn thought. How dare they question his commitment! Wasn't he risking life and limb to assure that the bulls were safely loaded in their chutes? Let them spend their time climbing from one chute to another while those miserable, ungrateful creatures tried to dislodge the man responsible for their sleek and powerful condition!

A minute later, Lynn was laughing at herself. She'd spent the past week trying to convince herself that she and Bryan were at loggerheads over something without form or substance. But all it took was for someone to question Bryan's integrity, and she was ready to defend him.

Why she felt that way, Lynn didn't know. It was enough to be able to look at him again without having her guard up. Not long ago they'd compromised, or threatened to compromise, their relationship. It had been a fluke, a combination of the close space, their near-naked bodies, the night.

It was once again night, but this time Lynn was in her one dressy riding outfit and Bryan's mind had to be everywhere but on her. If by chance she caught his eye, he wouldn't have the time or inclination to give her more than a quick nod.

Stop shying away from him, Lynn rebuked herself. Stop acting as if the two of you are adversaries. You don't have to let him kiss you again—you don't have to reach for him. The two of you can be friends.

Tonight, instead of asking Dee to act as a buffer between Bryan and herself, Lynn was waiting for him outside the foreman's trailer when the last animal had been returned to its corral. She watched his slow, studied walk as he approached her. Bryan was in tune with his surroundings. He was taking a reading of the rodeo grounds, assuring himself that he could lay down the mantle of responsibility for a few hours.

"Those humane officials," Lynn started. "Did they say why they were here? Did they take up much of your time?"

If Bryan was surprised to see her, he hid his reaction well. He jammed his hands into his back pockets and shook his head in resignation. "Not much. I'm used to it. When they hear things, it's their job to check it out."

"But, didn't they know how busy we are? The least they could have done was wait until we're—"

"We?" Bryan interrupted.

"All right." Lynn dropped her eyes. She was uncomfortably aware of his sensuality. She should have waited to approach him when there were others around. "It's your stock. I was just— It went well to-night, didn't it?"

Bryan continued to focus on her downcast eyes. "What did?" he asked.

"The rodeo," Lynn said. What was the matter with her? She couldn't put two words together, let alone carry on a coherent conversation. It was Bryan's fault, she decided. He had no right being so...attractive. "There weren't any major problems."

"No there weren't. Lynn, I want to change my clothes and then do a little record keeping before I turn in. Do you mind?"

"Of course not," Lynn said, hurt.

"I'm going to have to get some things from your trailer later." Bryan took a step, pulled his hand out of his pocket and reached for the door to the foreman's trailer. Lynn felt him slide by; she felt lonely.

Despite the risk, Lynn followed Bryan inside. The foreman's trailer was the same size as the Stone's, but because it didn't also serve as an office, there was a feeling of space. The feeling left as soon as the door swung shut behind her.

"We've been acting like fools around each other."

Bryan had reached for his shirt buttons; her words stopped him. "Fools?" he echoed.

"Maybe that's not the right word," Lynn amended. "I don't know how we've been acting. It's just that, Bryan, I don't feel natural around you. I'm on edge all the time."

Bryan jerked off his shirt, revealing naked flesh. "How should we feel around each other?"

Lynn had always believed Bryan to be honest and open, without deception, but if he was asking that question, challenging her because he needed to control the situation, she wasn't sure she could forgive him. "I don't know how we're supposed to feel around each other." Lynn's jaw clenched; she didn't try to hide the fact. "All I know is, I'm here tonight because I don't like things the way they are. I hoped we could put an end to that. But if you aren't going to help me—"

"What is it you want me to do?"

"I don't know. Darn it! I don't know." Lynn turned away. She was a breath away from walking out the door, and that was the last thing she wanted. Bryan stopped her.

"Don't leave." He'd caught her elbow. The light pressure turned her smoothly back around to face him. "I'm sorry, Lynn," he said softly. "I'm not very good at playing word games."

"Neither am I."

"You . . ." His hand slid to her wrist. "What was it you wanted to say?"

With her free hand, Lynn smoothed her hair away from her throat. She was unaware of Bryan's quick intake of breath in response. "I want us to be able to talk to each other. I want us to be comfortable around each other."

"We weren't comfortable the other night."

"I know." A little of the tension she'd brought into the trailer seeped out of Lynn. They were talking. At least something had been accomplished. "I don't know what happened that night. Or why." Although it cost her, she gently pulled her hand free. "Maybe it was a combination of things. I know . . ." Lynn swallowed. "I know I was being influenced by the night's mood, relief at having my ride over with. Feeling good about myself. Maybe too good," she laughed. That was only part of the story, but Lynn wasn't ready to admit, even to herself, that no other man could have evoked that response from her. "I guess we'll have to guard against that happening again."

Bryan sat down and started tugging on his boots. He could have asked Lynn to help him. It was a companionable gesture that those around the rodeo often did for each other. But Lynn would have to touch his calf, straddle his leg. And if she did that he wasn't sure he could keep his hands off her. He wasn't sure he wanted to. "You think it was an accident?"

"Do you?"

Despite having his question thrown back at him, Bryan had to admire Lynn for facing the situation more squarely than he. "No. I don't think it was an accident, Lynn," he told her. "And I don't think it had anything to do with the night or cramped quarters."

"What then?"

She was whispering, giving him proof of her uneasy emotional state. Bryan wanted to give her honesty. He was beginning to think he needed to give her himself. But that had never been his way. As long as he'd been able to bury himself in work, he'd been able to avoid emotional commitment. He'd slipped once and paid the price. He wasn't ready to take the risk again. Not until he knew more about her. And himself.

Lynn wasn't ready to give up. Bryan had to give her credit for that. "I believe in things I can touch and see. Work, commitment and responsibility."

When he looked at her, Lynn was smiling. "I think you know yourself very well, Bryan Stone."

"What about you?" Bryan asked. "How well do you know yourself?" Her flaxen hair slid forward again. This time Bryan brushed it back.

Lynn melted at his touch. But he'd asked a question; he was waiting for an answer. "Not well enough," was all she could say.

"I don't believe that. You aren't a little girl anymore."

No she wasn't. She was a woman with a woman's needs. "I think—I think maybe it's easier for you to find what you're about than it is for me." He'd returned to the task of removing his remaining boot, but the memory of his touch lingered. "You talk about work and responsibility. I can do that, too. But I also have to, if I'm being honest, talk about feelings."

"And what are you feeling?"

He wasn't concentrating on his boots anymore. Once again his gaze was on her. "Too much." Lynn laughed. "I feel so much when I'm around you." Lynn made the mistake of looking into his eyes. In them she found emotion to match her own. Still, she continued. "Women go around risking their sanity by involving their feelings in everything they do."

"Women?"

"All right," she amended angrily. "I'm the one who goes around risking my sanity. Is that what you want me to say?"

"I want you to say what's right for you." Bryan slid into a pair of tennis shoes without looking down at his feet.

How had the conversation taken this turn? Lynn had wanted them to talk, to find a road map to some kind of relationship, but this was too intense. "Not at the end of a long day," she told him.

Bryan got to his feet. The last thing he wanted to do was leave before this was settled, but he'd told her he still had work to do, and he didn't know what to say to make things right between them. "About your trailer... I shouldn't bother you long."

"Bother" was not the word Lynn would have used. Although he didn't ask for her company, she followed him outside and into the trailer she shared with Dee. While Bryan searched for something among the invoices, Lynn read the note from Dee she'd found on her bed.

"I don't know when she's going to be back," Lynn told Bryan. "All she says is, not to wait up for her."

"Out chasing cowboys again." The anger Lynn had heard earlier was no longer there. Instead Lynn thought she heard a kind of sorrow in Bryan's voice. "Someday she's going to fall in love. I hope she doesn't get hurt."

"You can't live her life for her, Bryan," Lynn whispered. She could have handled it more easily if he'd been angry. That way, maybe, the need to wrap her arms around him and pull him close wouldn't be so intense.

"So she tells me." Bryan had been studying the papers in his hand. Now he turned around, facing Lynn in the muted light cast by the lamp. Lynn heard him say something about childish squabbling that had turned into mutual respect. He looked so lonely.

This wasn't the flesh-and-blood man who'd orchestrated an entire rodeo earlier or even the man who knew her parents almost as well as she did. The man standing in front of her, with his head inclined toward her, seemed to be offering a promise of sensuality and love if she could just find a way to release it.

Still, Lynn didn't know how to begin, how to let him know he didn't have to be alone. She found his eyes, locked on to the message he was sending her and made the first move. The hand holding the papers he'd come in for dropped to his side. She took another step. Invoices and bills fluttered soundlessly to the floor.

Bryan touched her first. She felt his fingers cup her cheeks in a exquisitely gentle gesture. There was nothing controlling in his touch. He was, like her, asking questions.

But Lynn had no doubts about Bryan Stone. She'd worked side by side with him. She'd acknowledged the distance between them, understanding that intimacy, if it was to be cherished, needed to develop in its own time.

That time was now. Lynn had no knowledge of what the outcome might be, only that the journey had begun and, tonight, neither of them was going to pull back. She leaned forward, touching her fingers to his waist. Because she hadn't taken her eyes off him, she was able to read his every reaction. He was glad and shaken and in the grip of an emotion not easily extinguished. Lynn wouldn't ask him to kill that emotion. She had a like one to blend with his. Whether the fire resulted in ashes or lasting flames would only be determined in time.

Her mouth was sweet and gentle, passionate and probing. Bryan folded Lynn against him, marveling at how easy it was to tune himself to the beating of her heart. A kiss shouldn't mean this much. Bryan had kissed other women. A few times he'd even taken more when it was offered. When that had happened, he'd tried to tell himself that passion had a life span longer than one night, but before the dawn, he'd known that he'd deceived himself.

What he was feeling for Lynn Walker was different from anything he'd ever felt before. He was aware of the burning inside him, the instant response to her woman's body. But he was experiencing much more than a physical reaction. It wasn't just her body he wanted. Tonight Bryan wanted to make love to Lynn's mind and soul.

Bryan held Lynn in his arms, their lips recording and giving and sharing. And before the night was over, there might be no distinction left between the two of them.

He was certain that someday her passion for competing would claim her again, but meanwhile he would share what he could. While he could.

Lynn's hands slid upward from Bryan's waist, caressing his ribs, his arms, his shoulders, until finally she was clinging to his neck the way a drowning man clings to a lifeline. She heard nothing but his breathing; she saw nothing except his image; she had no memory of any taste beyond his lips. Where they were wasn't important. What was going on beyond these four thin walls belonged to another world.

There was only Bryan.

Lynn parted her lips more and pressed against his chest. His tongue was between her teeth, reaching deeper, taking, giving. She returned his passion in kind.

Tears stung Lynn's eyes but didn't shame her. Her body felt soft and flowing as if she might lose it. Still, she had no fear. If after tonight she changed, Lynn was ready for that. She needed him—only him. Together they could make something magical happen.

"Dee won't be back?" Bryan whispered.

"I don't think we'll see her before morning."

"Then we have the night?"

He was asking permission to make love to her. Lynn answered before she claimed his mouth again. "The night," she managed.

Bryan undressed her so slowly that Lynn felt as though her body was something to be worshiped. She believed he had so much more to offer. His body was a road map of his life. There were the scars, hard muscle, pale flesh where the sun hadn't touched. In nakedness he was magnificent.

His hands were in constant motion, covering her breasts, ribs, waist, stomach. He lowered his head and kissed her between her breasts.

When she had first reached for him, Lynn had been filled with tenderness and wonder and the excitement of the journey ahead of her. Now, standing naked before him, Lynn was losing herself in a fire she'd never believed her body capable of. She wanted his hands everywhere. She needed his lips to touch every inch of her body. She wanted to consume and be consumed. Explore and be explored.

Lynn wanted the night to go on forever.

Bryan was pressed against her, giving her access to all of him. Lynn accepted without hesitancy. Bryan was coming to her without artifice or deception. He had only himself to offer; the offer was being given freely.

Lynn took that offering as the most sacred of trusts.

"You feel so good," Bryan whispered. "I thought . . . I wasn't sure."

"What weren't you sure of?"

"Whether this would ever happen."

Lynn waited until Bryan had lifted her in his arms and laid her on the bed. "Neither was I," she told him as his weight on the bed pulled her toward him. Despite the cool night air, he was her warmth. His voice was the only sound she heard. "I didn't know if we'd ever—"

"Don't talk, Lynn. We can talk tomorrow."

A small chill momentarily stilled the flames. Was this all Bryan wanted? Was he asking for her body and not for all of her? Lynn pushed the question aside. Lovemaking, better than words, would show her what kind of man Bryan Stone was.

He was fire.

Lynn was lost in his touch. She'd thought she was ready for everything he was offering. But what she had felt while he was exploring her paled before what followed. He knew when to kiss her flesh with whispering fingers, when to slide his hands quickly over her sensitive thighs and when to linger on her breasts.

Because he was sure, Lynn became sure herself. She'd always thought a man's body sacred, an instrument to touch in wonder. But tonight she wasn't content to let Bryan take the lead. She needed to explore. She needed to let him bring her to fever pitch while she brought him to the brink of madness.

And finally, Lynn opened herself to him; became him and asked him to become her. Then she lost herself, not caring whether she'd ever find herself again. Every inch of her flesh had felt his imprint; now she was feeling him deep inside her. Absorbing him and going gladly where he led, going where she had never gone before. He gave her pleasure she'd never imagined. She was floating, flying, exploding. Then she joined him in his own explosion.

"I never knew," Bryan whispered. They were spent, resting together, still touching.

Lynn touched her tongue to his throat and tasted him. She took the taste deep inside her. "What didn't you know?"

"That it could be. Lynn, are you going to be all right?"

As long as Bryan was beside her, Lynn didn't believe anything dark could ever touch her again. "Oh, yes," she told him. "You have to believe that."

"I mean, could you be pregnant?"

Pregnant. His mind had already returned to the world while hers still remained lost inside him. Still, he'd asked a question that needed an answer. "No. I've been on the pill for years."

Bryan opened his eyes.

Lynn saw the question, the need for reaffirmation of what he had found during their lovemaking. She was able to give him that. "I'll explain it to you someday," she whispered. "Going on the pill was how I got rid of cramps and other things you don't want to hear about."

"I should have asked before."

"Bryan, I wouldn't have made love with you if I thought something might happen that neither of us was ready for." Lynn stopped. Her little speech made her sound practical, even calculating, when that wasn't what she was feeling at all. "I just wanted us to make love tonight. I didn't want to talk or think about anything else."

Bryan propped himself up on his elbow. "Was that all this was?"

Somehow she'd said the wrong thing. Bryan wanted verification that he'd been more than body for her tonight. She could tell him that without reservation. She still felt more of him than she did of herself. It could be hours, days, weeks, a lifetime maybe before she felt differently.

"Of course not, Bryan," she told him. "But I don't want to push this. Can't we take it one step at a time?"

One step at a time. That was a pace Bryan believed he could handle. "I hope so, Lynn," he whispered. He ran a finger over her hip, enjoying her quick response. He hadn't given her everything he had to give yet. He didn't know how long that might take, but they had the night.

Chapter Nine

Morning flowed peacefully over the rodeo grounds and made its gentle intrusion on the sleeping lovers. Bryan woke first, waiting for the world to come back into focus. This time he accepted the warm, quiet body next to his without question. He understood that as the hours went on, he would come to wonder at the miracle that had brought Lynn to him last night, but for these few precious moments he could believe that everything was right.

He could believe that neither of them would question whether they'd be able to join their separate lives and beliefs and commitments as completely as their bodies had joined. "I could love you, Lynn." It was more thought than sound. The simple words vibrated through Bryan, shaking him with their totality. Lynn Walker was no illusion, no temporary force. She'd always been part of his life. The forces that had shaped him shaped her as well. She had no ties to a world completely beyond his comprehension. He wouldn't have to introduce her to a life-style foreign to her.

And yet, just because their roots came from the same place didn't mean they would grow together. If he'd been younger or more innocent, Bryan might have believed love capable of surmounting all obstacles, but life had taught him different. He knew Lynn was embarked on a search for identity, for purpose, for something to commit herself to. He would never stand in the way of her goals; that wasn't love.

Bryan turned away from Lynn and slid out of bed. He walked, naked, to the small window in the trailer door and looked out. A teenager was pushing a loaded wheelbarrow toward one of the stables. A watering truck was already dampening the exercise oval. Dee would be back soon. It was time for him to return to the world he'd created for himself.

Lynn clung to sleep for a few more minutes, but because there was no one to share that innocent state with, she finally surrendered to reality. On an intellectual level, Lynn understood that Bryan had responsibilities and work that required attention. Still, she didn't want him to leave her yet.

"Another pancake breakfast?" she asked as a trio of cowboys tromped by talking loudly. "Don't they fix anything else at these rodeos?"

"I don't think so." Bryan had pulled on his jeans and was buttoning his shirt. "That's one of the best things about going home. Eating something different." The quick smile that stripped the years from his face faded. "We didn't do much talking last night."

"I know." Lynn smiled. She knew the day would be a long one for her, that she would have many emotional questions to face, but she'd worry about that later. Now she needed nothing more than to drink in the awareness of her lover's body. She remembered everything about him; she could paint his every line and curve. She knew where his flesh was perfect and where his life-style had made a permanent mark on him. She wasn't repelled by his scars. They were part of him. Maybe the next time she touched those scars, she could tell him how she felt.

"I'd like us to be together again tonight."

Lynn nodded, feeling herself soften once more. Tonight. The word had magic and promise. Yes, she wanted his lovemaking. She needed to again explore the places he could take her to and the totality her body was capable of. But lovemaking was only part of it. She'd come to think of him as her lover, but that touched only the surface. A lover takes his partner's body and plays it, molds it, creates something new out of the old. But a lover doesn't touch the heart of his partner unless more than flesh and bone are involved.

And much more than Lynn's flesh had gone to bed with Bryan last night. She'd given him her body, loved having that gift to give, and taken what he'd given in return. But it went deeper than that. Maybe tonight when he fulfilled his promise, she would understand more. "I'd like that," she told him shyly.

Lynn hadn't gotten out of bed by the time Bryan left. She was sitting up reaching around for her discarded clothes when the door opened. Dee blinked, but for a minute she didn't say anything. Finally she said, "I saw Bryan leaving. I take it you got my note."

Lynn nodded. Once Dee had said she hoped something would happen between Bryan and Lynn, but Lynn couldn't be sure how her best friend would react to knowing that she and Bryan were lovers. "Where were you?" she asked as she pulled on her jeans.

"It's a long story." Sighing, Dee collapsed on her bed. "It took me a couples of hours, but I finally got a hold of Bullet. I hate busy signals!"

"Bullet?" Lynn blinked. "Isn't he still in Texas? What did you want to talk to him for?"

Dee shrugged before flopping back on her pillow. "I got lonely for the sound of his voice. I wanted to hear how he'd done, whether he got there all right. All those sisterly things."

"You aren't his sister," Lynn pointed out.

"Don't," Dee groaned. "I'm too tired to play semantic games. I just needed to talk to him that's all. It took forever to get through to the rodeo there. And then I had to hang around this stupid pay phone waiting for him to call me back. By then—" Lynn thought she detected a catch in Dee's voice, but with the next words it was gone. "After we talked, I knew I couldn't sleep so I went for a long walk."

"You've been up all night? Dee? Are you all right?"

What might have been a smile if she wasn't already half asleep touched Dee's mouth. "I am now. He did great. Took first place."

"And that makes you feel good?" Lynn pressed. Dee and her brother?

"Not so much the first place, although that was the icing on the cake. I miss him, Lynn. Isn't that something? I really miss him."

Lynn left Dee alone after that. It was hard to get used to the idea that there was something more than friendship between Dee and Bullet, but then all the time she was growing up, Lynn had never once linked herself with Bryan. Things changed. People changed.

She wanted to talk to Bryan about what Dee had said, but the time never seemed right. Tonight, she kept reminding herself, they'd be able to talk. In the meantime, Lynn tried to concentrate on working White Moon. Exercise did what was necessary. Within

a few minutes of getting on White Moon's back, Lynn
was absorbed. The routine of circling the barrels had
become part of her. Any awkwardness, any hesitancy
she'd felt about her skills no longer existed. She was,
she could admit without conceit, good. Maybe good
enough for the brass ring and everything that went
with it. This morning Lynn had no doubts about her
decision to concentrate on competing instead of
opening her riding and training school. The school
would have paid the bills. Competing would do that
and a great deal more, if she allowed it to become her
life.

When she'd finished working with White Moon,
Lynn spent some time watching the practice sessions
of a few of the other barrel racers. Because she'd
stopped seeing the other women as simply her competition, she was able to strike up conversations with
several of them. One spent as much time trying to sell
a couple of horses as she did preparing for that night's
event. Another racer, a slender girl who didn't look
strong enough to go the distance, was obviously torn
between her desire to compete and meeting her
fiancé's demands on her time. Lynn's favorite was the
young mother who settled her toddler in front of her
and let the little one handle the reins. "That's what my
mother did for me," the woman explained. "She figured if I was old enough to sit up, I was ready to get
used to the feel of a horse."

Lynn watched the young mother for a long time,
trying to picture herself in a similar position. When
and if she had a family, would she want to continue
competing? And more important, would her husband
and children be able to accommodate the demanding
life-style it required?

She was still asking herself that question late that afternoon when the rodeo secretary found her. The heavy, middle-aged woman was so out of breath from running that it was several minutes before Lynn understood what had her so upset. When she did understand, Lynn would have given a year out of her life not to have heard the words.

Bullet had been injured. He was now in a Dallas hospital, condition unknown. Lynn's mother, who had asked that the message be relayed to Lynn, was trying to decide whether she should fly to him today or wait until they knew more.

Lynn sagged against the nearest fence, needing something to support her. "How long ago did you get the message?" she asked, wondering at the calm in her voice.

"I just got off the phone with your mother," the secretary told her. "She said—she said she didn't want to stay on the line while I tried to reach you. She wants you to call her back."

As if Lynn could think of anything else. Lynn left the secretary behind and sprinted across the grounds. Quickly she dialed home with trembling fingers.

"I don't know how bad it is," Carol explained after picking up the phone on the first ring. "That cowboy Bullet has been traveling with called. He said he hasn't been allowed in to see Bullet yet. He did say—" Carol's voice caught "—that Bullet was conscious and aware of a lot that was going on. That's all I know, honey. I've been trying to get through to the hospital myself, but I can't seem to get hooked up with anyone who knows anything."

Lynn insisted on trying to contact the hospital herself. After being put on hold twice, she was finally switched over to the emergency room. According to the records, Bullet had spent an hour in the emergency room before going in for surgery. Despite what the word "surgery" did to Lynn's nerves, she forced herself to concentrate while the person talking to her explained that an operation had been necessary to repair Bullet's spleen. His condition was listed as serious. He was now in recovery and wouldn't be able to talk to anyone before morning at least. When Lynn relayed that information to her mother, she could only say a silent prayer of thanks that Carol had her son and daughter-in-law around. Chet came on the line to reassure Lynn.

After hanging up, Lynn slumped into the nearest chair. The rodeo secretary was clucking sympathetically, but Lynn barely managed to mutter a reply to her concerned questions. Her mother had family around, but Lynn felt more alone than she had in years.

"HE'S GOING TO BE ALL RIGHT," she told Bryan five minutes later. She clung to him, taking strength from the strong arms wrapped around her, from the quick way he'd dismissed what he'd been doing and concentrated on her. "That blamed brother of mine is too tough for anything bad to happen to him."

"Do you want to go to him?"

"Yes. No. By the time I got there...I don't know," Lynn groaned, hating the indecision she was feeling. It shouldn't be that hard to decide what to do, but the fact was, there wouldn't be anything Lynn could do even if she flew to Dallas. What made sense was for her mother to go and for Lynn to wait for word. Still, sitting around doing nothing was driving her crazy. "I don't know what to do, Bryan."

They were still discussing the pros and cons of an expensive flight that might accomplish nothing when Dee found them. Even trapped in her concern and fear, Lynn hadn't forgotten that Dee had spent last night waiting to hear Bullet's voice. Her mind spun in circles trying to find a way of gently breaking the news. Unfortunately Bryan spoke first.

Dee's tanned face was instantly leeched of all its color. "Bullet," she said. "Bullet's hurt."

"As far as we know, a bronc fell on him," Bryan explained. "We'll know more after Lynn's mom gets there."

"I'm going."

"What?" Bryan looked at his sister as if she'd lost her mind. "Look, Lynn hasn't decided whether it'd do her any good to go. Whatever do you—"

"Will you shut up!" Dee snapped. "I can't—I can't just stay here."

"Are you sure?" Lynn asked gently. She was still concerned for her brother, but because she could feel Dee's fear and tension, she had no choice but to focus on that. "There probably isn't anything you can do."

"I can be there. Lynn, I have to go."

Maybe there was something Dee could do, after all, Lynn thought. If Bullet was feeling even a little of what Dee obviously was, he would much rather have Dee standing beside his bed than his sister. "Go then," Lynn told her softly.

If Dee was going to leave soon, then it was up to Lynn to take over her friend's responsibilities. Bryan was still asking confused questions as the women walked away. "Explain it to him, please," Dee asked once they were out of earshot. "He doesn't know what to think."

Lynn turned back toward Bryan. He was staring after them, his body part and parcel of his surroundings. It took every ounce of strength in Lynn's body not to return to him. "I'm not sure I know what to think, either," Lynn told her friend. "Are you in love with Bullet?"

"I don't know," Dee groaned. "I don't know what I'm feeling these days."

"But it isn't what you've ever felt around him before, is it?"

Dee shook her head. "Last night, when I finally got a hold of him, he told me how excited he was. He was feeling better about his performances than he had in a long time. He felt good. I felt good for him. I knew he was glad to have me to share that with. That's all I know, Lynn."

"I understand," Lynn reassured her. The strange thing was, Lynn really did understand. Before last night, before making love to Bryan, she might not have.

THE REST OF THE DAY PASSED in a blur of activity. Dee was able to make a plane reservation for ten that night, which gave her time to explain what Lynn would have to do in her absence before hurrying to pack. "I shouldn't be doing this to you," Dee groaned after Lynn had insisted on driving Dee to the airport. "You're going to be so busy. How are you going to have time to compete?"

"Why don't you let me worry about that? Besides, it isn't as if you're never coming back. Get my brother out of that darn hospital and back on his feet. That's

going to be a lot harder than my holding down the fort
for you.''

A FEW WEEKS AGO, Lynn would have felt over-
whelmed by what she'd agreed to take on, but because she'd been traveling with the Stones, she
understood most of what Dee was telling her. Still, it
amazed her that Dee had taken on the amount of responsibility she had.

THAT EVENING'S RODEO was over by the time Lynn
returned from taking Dee to the tiny airport and the
private pilot who would take her to Portland for her
connection. She wearily trudged back to the trailer and
shut herself inside. Although her body ached for sleep,
Lynn's mind refused to let go. She was worried about
Bullet and still getting used to Dee's need to be with
him. She hadn't had time to figure out how she was
going to juggle her new duties with competing, but
that concern could be dealt with tomorrow.

She'd barely had time to undress when she heard a
soft knock. "I'm so glad to see you," she whispered
to Bryan once she was in the haven of his arms. "I still
can't believe today happened."

"You've faced a crisis before, Lynn. You'll get
through this one." Bryan could feel the exhaustion in
Lynn's body and responded with a concern he didn't
know he was capable of. The last time he'd felt anything close to this emotion, he'd been helping a man
he loved say goodbye to life. Lynn was warm and
alive, but she needed him, too. Knowing that, accept-
ing that burden, wanting it even, bound them together in ways Bryan didn't yet understand.

What Bryan did with words and gestures and sweet caresses took Lynn beyond concern for her brother. He reassured her that there was nothing she could do to help Bullet tonight. How long and what form Bullet's recovery would take they didn't know. And punishing herself emotionally about that while she waited wouldn't change anything. Bryan showed her that she needed to focus on what was good and right in her life, to make herself strong enough for whatever came to pass.

Bryan was what was good and right in her life.

Gently he reached for her. Lovingly he gave her proof of what she was capable of feeling.

That night Bryan led her softly through a thousand emotions, stopping to savor each one as it unfolded. He held himself in check and put her needs before his. His lips on her mouth, breasts and shoulders demanded no more than what she was capable of giving in return. He understood her slow responses, her brief backing away, her final total surrender.

He took his reward in the words she gave him when they'd spent themselves. "You're beautiful," Lynn whispered. "I had no idea you could be so beautiful."

"It wasn't me, Lynn," he whispered back. "Whatever you felt, you're the one who's responsible for that."

Lynn shook her head before reaching over to run her lips along Bryan's collarbone. "I didn't think we'd make love tonight," she told him. "I wanted you here. There was never any doubt of that. But I thought I wasn't going to be able to give you anything."

"You did, sweetheart." Bryan barely heard himself say the word. Tonight was for Lynn. "You made it right for me."

"Did I?" Lynn tried to laugh at the question that didn't need to be asked, but her mind was on what Bryan had just called her. Sweetheart. What a beautiful, wonderful word.

They fell asleep locked in each other's arms and minds. Lynn had no idea what time it was when she became aware of her world again. She slid her fingers through Bryan's rich hair, listened to his quiet breathing, studied his strong profile. It was night. There was no need to hold anything back.

Lynn was in love. In the middle of the night she could surround herself with this new wonder. She could pull it around her and marvel at its powerful spell. Bryan had been the perfect lover for a woman who didn't know how to ask for what she needed. Who hadn't know what she needed until he showed it to her. He'd sensed her every emotion and answered her every need.

But she was also afraid of loving a man who knew what he wanted out of life, who had seen the boundaries of his world and accepted them willingly. Her goals went no farther than a well-trained horse and a skill she'd been born with.

THEIR MORNING BEGAN AT DAWN. Lynn was in the shower when Bryan received word that one of the drivers was in the county jail sleeping off too much celebration from the night before. Although it would leave him shorthanded, Bryan had no doubts about what he was doing when he left word at the jail that the driver was out of a job. This wasn't Jim's first run-in with a bottle. In fact, Bryan had kept him on the payroll despite warning him twice that he was skating on thin ice. Bryan hated giving up on Jim, but the driver would never learn to be accountable for his actions if someone was always picking up the pieces and making excuses for him.

Bryan's immediate problem was finding a replacement fast so that Stone Stock could get to Reno. By volunteering to drive, Lynn provided him with a solution. Although Bryan pointed out that jockeying a trailer around took a great deal of experience, Lynn explained that growing up on a ranch had taught her how to drive anything with wheels. "Bryan, you can't pull someone qualified out of a hat. Why should you try when I'll do it?"

"It's a long way to Nevada," Bryan tried to point out. "And there's no power steering." Lynn was dressed in her usual attire. Only the damp hair clinging to her neck kept her from completing the cowgirl image. That and Bryan's memory of her soft, giving body.

"Then we'd better get on the road," Lynn told him. "Dee knows where we're headed. She'll try to reach us."

AFTER A TEN-HOUR DRIVE, the caravan spent the night at a ranch belonging to a friend of Bryan's. There was no chance for Lynn and Bryan to get together, but just having him near was enough. He smiled when she smiled at him. He knew when she needed a touch, a whispered word of encouragement.

They reached Reno in the middle of a hot afternoon. The caravan avoided the streets lined with casinos, but Lynn didn't mind. She'd never understood the appeal of gambling. Besides, since there might be a message waiting for them from Dee, she was eager to get to the rodeo grounds.

Lynn jockeyed her truck and trailer into position, but there was barely time to stretch her aching muscles before going to work. The animals had been cooped up for the better part of two days and needed room to move. Lynn jumped down from the cab and hurried around to unlock the rear gate. With the help of a couple of teenagers employed by the rodeo committee, Lynn had the horses unloaded and into a common corral by the time Bryan had emptied the truck holding the roping calves. Then together they hurried to the office.

The secretary, a harried woman who let Bryan and Lynn know she'd had no idea the job would be this hard when she took it, had taken notes on what Dee had said. If the secretary had gotten the information right, Bullet was out of intensive care and complaining because they wouldn't let him have a real meal.

"What about his injuries?" Lynn asked. "Dee must have said something."

The secretary waved her hand in the air. "Oh, she did, but I didn't get it all down. Some internal injuries. You have no idea how hectic it's been around here."

"You must remember something," Lynn pressed. Her eyes burned from hours of staring at blacktop. If she had to sit anymore today, her backbone would probably disintegrate. Lynn had a pretty good idea what the secretary had to do, but the woman had to have known that the message was important.

"No, I don't," the secretary snapped. "I can't do everything, but no one seems to understand that. This is not an answering service, you know."

Bryan muttered something under his breath before pointing out that the secretary wasn't nearly as busy as she was going to be once the cowboys started to arrive. "Did you happen to get a phone number?" he asked tersely. "My sister must have said where she's staying."

"There." The secretary pointed at a stack of papers. "It's in there somewhere. While you're looking for it, I'm going to get myself a soft drink." She was gone before Bryan could do more than glare at her.

"Don't say anything," Lynn warned. "There's nothing you can say that I haven't been thinking. Where did they get her, anyway?"

"You don't want to know." Bryan held a coffee-stained scrap of paper. "That's a Texas area code. Why don't you give it a try." He glanced at another piece of paper, paused, and then read it thoroughly. "This is for us, too. From Rusty. More problems."

"What kind of problems?"

Rusty's youngest daughter was talking about getting married, so he and his wife were going to try to talk sense into the seventeen-year-old. "This says both Jagger and Tate will be here to cover for him. I don't know. The last time I saw those two, they'd both had too much to drink. The note's from the rodeo committee. They haven't seen either Jagger or Tate yet." Bryan dropped the sheet of paper onto the desk. "They want to know what I'm going to do about it. This is not my job. The committee contracts with the clowns. As if there isn't enough to worry about," Bryan muttered before leaving.

Fortunately Lynn was able to reach Dee at the motel number she'd been given. Dee's story was much more complete than the one the secretary had given them. "I think we're going to get him out of here tomorrow," Dee explained. "Your mom's raising as much of a fuss about that as Bullet. If I was the hospital staff, I'd be happy to be rid of them both."

"How is he?" Lynn asked. "Is he going to be able to rodeo again?"

Dee sounded a little shaky. "As long as he's alive, he'll rodeo. You know how he feels about that. The doctor wants him to lay off until next season, but I don't think your brother is listening. I've tried to talk to him, but all he can think about is the money he's losing." Dee sighed. "He's going to have to stay with your mom for a while, but he isn't going to be there a minute longer than he has to."

Lynn hated the miles separating her from Dee. "What about you? How are you holding up?"

"I'll make it, Lynn. As long as Bullet's all right, I'll make it."

Lynn had to be content with that explanation. She'd started out the door when the phone rang again. Because the secretary hadn't returned, Lynn felt compelled to answer it.

An hour later Lynn was still manning the phones and the secretary was nowhere to be seen. She was rummaging through the avalanche of papers on the desk looking for some information the current caller needed when a slender man dressed in a navy blue suit walked in. He paced until Lynn was free.

"Where's Margaret?"

"If Margaret is the rodeo secretary, your guess is as good as mine," Lynn answered shortly. "She should have been back long ago."

"Darn it. Look, don't you move. Someone's got to hold this place together."

Lynn tried to point out that she already had more than enough to do, but the man was out the door. A few minutes later, cowboys started filing in asking questions about where they could set up their campers, where they could find feed for their horses, were there messages from wives or girlfriends, and either complaining or expressing pleasure over the animals they'd been paired with. Before Lynn knew it, the afternoon was over and she was starving. Margaret was still nowhere in sight.

Lynn barely noticed when the man in the suit returned. Although someone else was already waiting to talk to Lynn, the man pushed ahead of him. "Margaret quit," he announced.

"So?" Lynn's taut nerves made it impossible for her to be as civil as she should be. "Who's going to take her place?"

The man shrugged. "I'll try to get someone in here tomorrow if you can't do it. This is the biggest mess I've ever seen. We're going to be lucky if we have a clown tonight and now this! I can't believe the way this thing is being run!"

Lynn stopped the tirade. "I can't do this tomorrow." The phone rang; she ignored it. "I'm supposed to compete tonight, but I don't know how that's going to be possible. And I already have another job." No wonder she hadn't seen Bryan. He was doing Dee's work as well as his own.

The immaculately dressed man spent several minutes trying to convince Lynn that she was right for the glamorous job of rodeo secretary, but Lynn caught on. Unless she was mistaken, he was the head of the rodeo committee and, in that capacity, responsible for making sure there was a secretary on hand. He was also the one who should be dealing with the clown problems. The man had made a mistake with his first choice for secretary and was trying to get himself off the hook by drafting Lynn. But Lynn wouldn't cooperate.

After letting the man know that, Lynn fielded one last phone call and left the phone off the hook. She was walking out the office door when she noticed that the powerfully built young man who'd been in the office was following her.

"I'm looking for Mr. Stone," he told her. "I understand he's been asking for a clown."

"Are you one?"

"That's what they tell me." The young man stuck out his hand. "Jagger Duncan. I would have been here earlier but . . . You don't want to hear what happened to my radiator."

Feeling almost lightheaded now that she was out of the crowded office, Lynn linked arms with the young man and headed toward Bryan's trailer. She was actually smiling, something she hadn't thought she'd be able to do today.

The smile faded as soon as Lynn heard Bryan. He was just outside his trailer standing toe-to-toe with a tall man who was badly in need of a shave. Both men's body language told Lynn everything she needed to know about how the two were relating. Despite the distance separating them, Lynn was able to make out every word they were saying to each other. Between curses from the tall man and terse commands from Bryan, it was clear that Bryan was talking to the other overdue clown.

"I need you sober, Tate. If you hadn't pickled your brains, you would know what kind of danger you're putting those cowboys in by not being sharp in the arena. I've never had anyone killed at one of my rodeos. I'm not going to let it happen tonight."

"I know my job, Bryan. One drink. No one gets fired for that."

"It wasn't one drink." Bryan leaned forward. "I'm sorry but you aren't making any money tonight."

The man tried to lean forward as Bryan had done but almost lost his balance. "Rusty..."

Bryan sighed. "The last time we went through this, Rusty backed me up. You've got to get some help with your drinking, Tate. Until you do, you don't have any business clowning."

"You can't do that."

"I might not want to, but I have to." Bryan shook his head and turned away.

"That's it? Just like that?" Tate started to weave after Bryan, but when Bryan turned around, the tall man pulled himself to a halt. A second later he sidled away.

Bryan spotted Lynn. In the space of a second, the anger, disappointment and resentment he'd been feeling dissolved. He'd heard that Lynn had been pressed into service, but he'd been too busy to check how she was doing. Obviously she'd survived. He paid no attention to the man with her. "I'm sorry it had to turn out that way," he told her. "But I can't have a clown in the arena unless he knows exactly why he's there."

"My sentiments exactly," the powerfully built young man broke in. "I've worked with Tate for the better part of a year now. If he'd just get a handle on his problem he'd do fine."

Somehow Bryan was able to tear his attention away from Lynn.

"I might not have Tate's nerves," Jagger said. "But I'll give you your money's worth. And I can work alone. I've done it before."

"I don't think we have any choice. Look, I'll put extra men in the arena to help. You have no idea how glad I am to see you. And you." Bryan smiled at Lynn. "I see you got out of there."

But not for long. After a quick kiss and a moment in Bryan's arms, Lynn had to leave. Much of what she promised Dee she'd handle still needed to be done. The rodeo would begin in a couple of hours, and if she didn't hurry...

Any thoughts Lynn had of being able to compete tonight went out the window. Because there was no one to handle the secretary's job, Lynn took charge of figuring the cowboys' point standings and managing the prize money. She wasn't surprised to learn that the rodeo committee's bookkeeping left a lot to be desired.

And yet as hard as Lynn worked, it seemed that Bryan was working even harder. Just before the rodeo was to begin, the arena director was thrown from his horse and broke his arm. Bryan turned his loading chute duties over to his foreman and took over the responsibility of keeping the arena clear.

Lynn was sitting with the announcer helping him keep the different contestants straight during the bronc riding event when she realized it was Bryan who'd just

ridden past. She could only shake her head in wonder. He was obviously pinch-hitting as a pick up man,
racing alongside a bucking horse, guiding his stallion
close to those dangerously sharp hooves so the cowboy could climb behind Bryan instead of risk being
trampled by landing on the ground.

Bryan remained in the arena throughout the saddle
and bareback events. Despite the dust that rose in a
continuous wave, Lynn saw his clenched teeth, his intense eyes. In a few hours, he would feel the effects of
the exertion he was putting himself through, but for
now he had no existence beyond helping cowboys out
of potentially dangerous situations.

It's all on your shoulders, isn't it, Lynn thought. She
wasn't thinking about the responsibilities she'd taken
on today. She wasn't thinking ahead to what might or
might not happen when she and Bryan were alone
again. All she cared about was Bryan.

Lynn was shaking by the time the rodeo was over.
She could sense her physical exhaustion, but that
wasn't what had stripped the strength from her legs.
This place, these smells, these sounds, this was Bryan
Stone's life. He belonged here as surely as a child be-
longs in its parents' arms. Nothing, no one, would ever
take him from here.

If she was to become part of Bryan Stone's future,
she would have to accept that.

BRYAN HADN'T BEEN ABLE to spot Lynn once the lights
over the arena had been extinguished, and there'd been
too many demands on his time for him to go looking
for her. Anger and frustration made it possible for him
to ignore his own exhaustion. Lynn should have been
competing tonight. She had that right; that was what

she'd come here for. But she'd taken on responsibilities that should have been someone else's, and her own dreams had been placed on hold. He wondered if she'd ever be able to forgive him for it.

He found her in the trailer, already in bed. He didn't bother turning on the light but shed his boots in the dark, listening to her breathing, guessing that she wasn't asleep but might be feeling her disappointment so keenly that she didn't trust herself to speak. Finally he couldn't take it anymore. "Blast Dee."

Lynn turned toward him. "Dee? What does she have to do with anything?"

"If she'd been here, doing her job, you wouldn't have been playing Superwoman." Bryan sat on the side of the bed but stopped short of touching Lynn. Once he did that, there might be no talking, and they needed to talk. "Dee didn't have to go after Bullet. Your mother was there."

"She cares," Lynn whispered. "I understand."

"Maybe. But my sister put herself first. And you're the one who's paying the price."

"You don't know what you're talking about." Lynn had almost been asleep when Bryan came in, but now she was awake. Awake and frightened. They were going to fight, and she didn't know why. "It's not a matter of Dee putting herself first. I wanted her to go. She feels something for Bullet. I hope he feels something for her. Bryan, they need time together. If you're going to blame anyone, blame me."

"All right. I do blame you for not competing tonight. For sacrificing yourself." Bryan reached for her, but there was no tenderness in his grip. "I can tell you what's going to happen. You're going to burn yourself out before this darn rodeo is over. You're going to hate what you're doing and resent not being able to compete and—"

"How do you know what I'm feeling?" Lynn interrupted. "You're throwing all kinds of things at me. All right. So I'm not happy with the way things went today. It isn't the end of the world."

"You have to get back on White Moon. That's what you're here for."

Is that what Bryan thought? Did she seem so selfish? Did he think she didn't care about him and Dee? "Don't make my decisions for me, Bryan."

"Someone has to. Otherwise something's going to happen."

"What's going to happen?" Lynn prompted. She could have pulled free, but she forced herself to remain still. Bryan hadn't said enough. She still didn't know where his anger was coming from. "What's going to happen to me?"

Bryan's answer came from deep inside him. "You're going to take off again."

"I'm going to do what?"

"Take off. That's what you did when you weren't happy living in Harney county.

Lynn was hurt. Bryan had to know that a great deal had changed since those days. Things had happened to her, things that had to do with the both of them. Unless Bryan told her he didn't want her around, she couldn't imagine leaving him.

"That's right." Her words were heavy with sarcasm. "Whenever things don't go my way, I take off. Is that what you believe?"

"I believe—" Bryan said with his hand on her shoulder "—that you have a dream and nothing is going to stand in your way. Even me."

"You'd let me go?" Lynn didn't want to hear the answer.

"I'd make you go. If that's what it would take for you to fulfill your dream, I'd make you go." Before he'd finished speaking, Bryan had gotten to his feet. He turned from her, glimpsing a corner of the sky through the window. He could make out the pale white moon but only one star.

"Lynn? I'm doing what I want with my life. It has to be the same for you."

When she didn't respond, Bryan took a step closer to the window. In three more nights the moon would be full. Bryan had always been drawn to the moon when it was at its peak, but tonight he saw nothing except the solitary star. Tonight, that lonely star was him.

Chapter Ten

For a long while Lynn could think of nothing to say. She heard the caring in Bryan's voice and that frightened her. She felt her silent answer and that frightened her, too.

He didn't want her to leave him. She couldn't imagine ever turning her back on what he'd offered her in a few short weeks. But it was too much too fast. Lynn had never before experienced the intensity of emotion Bryan was able to excite in her. If she'd been eighteen, she would have surrendered to the current, aware of nothing except each moment. She wouldn't have seen distant cliffs or even been aware that the current could leave her dashed against ungiving rocks.

But Lynn was no longer a newcomer to the world of love. She had learned caution. She knew that, no matter how strong the current, she must keep her eyes open. She was the only one responsible for controlling her journey. "You don't know what I'm going to do," she told Bryan. "And neither do I."

Bryan should have braced himself for what Lynn was telling him. He was a fool if he expected her to throw herself into his arms and promise undying love.

Just because he'd fallen in love didn't mean she would return the emotion.

Obviously Lynn had no intention of turning her life and her heart over to him. She'd given him what she could, which in the end was nothing. He had to accept that his heart was on a solitary journey. She didn't love him. Her concern, as it should be, was with defining the direction her life needed to take.

"Just do one thing, will you, Lynn," he heard himself say. "Let me know before you take off. Dee turned her back on her responsibilities. The business is going to be in trouble if you go, too."

"The business. Of course," Lynn said through her pain. What a fool she'd been to believe that their two nights together had changed him in any profound way. Bryan was married to his business. "No, Bryan, I won't leave you in the lurch. But, if you'll take a minute to be honest, you'll have to admit that Dee didn't simply wander off because she had something more interesting to do."

"Maybe," Bryan conceded. He hadn't understood his sister's sudden interest in Lynn's brother, but at least she'd exchanged one responsibility for another rather than running off in pursuit of fun. "Did you get to talk to her more than that one time?" he asked.

Lynn explained that the rodeo office phone had rung off the hook all day. Even if Dee had tried to call, she probably couldn't have gotten through. From there the conversation changed to a discussion of what needed to be done in the morning. Before Bryan had come in, Lynn had been a breath away from total exhaustion. But now she was awake, nerves on edge. She couldn't sleep. She could talk, but not about what mattered.

Finally Lynn ran out of things to say. She'd been promised there would be a replacement secretary there in the morning. Maybe, if the woman knew what she was doing, Lynn could find time to compete in the evening. Lynn flopped back on the bed, hands behind her head, chest rising and falling slowly as sleep once again tried to claim her. She could hear Bryan moving around as he got ready for bed. Would he reach for her? Did he want to make love? Did she?

Bryan sat watching the gentle rise and fall of Lynn's breasts against her thin nightshirt. She was exquisite, breathing in rhythm with her life. It tore him apart to know that one day a warm wind would blow across them, a wind capable of taking Lynn with it.

He couldn't imagine going back to what he'd been before she'd entered his life. Yes, he'd fought pain and loneliness when Heather left him, but even when what he felt for Heather had run hot and fast through him, he'd always known she was a stranger to his world.

It wasn't that way with Lynn. She was ranch born and raised. She understood the cold hibernation of winter, the ageless promise of spring, the dulling heat that was part of summer. The seasons were part of them both.

But Lynn had left once and even though she'd come back, she was still restless, still searching. Someday, maybe soon, either Lynn's goals or her restlessness would make her leave him.

Bryan didn't reach for Lynn. Instead he waited until he was sure that she was asleep and then slid into the other bed. He tried to make his mind go blank and when that didn't work, he tried to concentrate on the responsibilities that would claim him in the morning. Nothing mattered without Lynn. Or if it did, the passion was gone. She, who had been on the edge of his existence for as long as he could remember, was now at its center.

Bryan decided he was a fool. He dozed fitfully but true sleep never came. Hours later, when the warm weight joined him he instantly knew who was there. Bryan reached for Lynn without asking, without questioning.

Lynn called herself a fool. She'd been able to fall asleep. Certainly her body had been tired enough to keep her in that state until morning. But her mind and heart didn't heed what her body was trying to tell her.

Lynn was lonely; she hated her aloneness. She and Bryan hadn't fought, not really. She'd convinced herself that Bryan hadn't touched her earlier because he knew how tired she was. Lynn appreciated his consideration, but she could tell by his breathing that he was only dozing. If she let him know...

Bryan reached for her before she'd pulled the sheet over herself. His touch was the only affirmation Lynn needed. Coming to him had been the right thing to do.

"I think I understand—" Bryan whispered "—about your brother and my sister. You're right. Dee didn't have any choice but to go to him."

"What changed your mind?" Lynn asked. Her hands were on him; she no longer cared about the reasons why they hadn't been together earlier.

"Sometimes." Bryan stopped long enough to taste and touch her. "Sometimes people simply have to be together."

"Even if it means going to Texas?"

"Even if nothing has been decided between them."

Wordlessly Bryan eased the nightshirt off Lynn. Then he caressed her breasts gently, until Lynn felt the pressure building throughout her. She reached for him, needing to give as much as he was giving. His stomach fascinated her as did the flesh over his ribs. To the outside world he was rawhide. His dark eyes told nothing of what he carried in his heart. Only those he loved—and those who loved him—knew better. Tonight he was opening himself to her. Now, at least, their separate goals and responsibilities didn't exist. His soft lips found her chin and traveled upward. Lynn was smiling as their lips touched. She would take these minutes. She would ask for no tomorrows.

They made love silently. But there was no savage intensity. Lynn knew she wasn't the only one holding back. They gave each other their bodies and the gift was wonderful. But because the outcome was too uncertain, she sensed Bryan, too, kept something of himself in reserve.

THE MAN IN THE SUIT had been half right. He had managed to round up a secretary to replace the one who had walked off the job, but the replacement had never been to a rodeo, let alone handled the behind-the-scenes operation of one.

Fortunately, because it was the second day of the rodeo, most of the work had already been done. Lynn gave the woman a cram course and told her where she could be found if an emergency developed.

Considering everything that could have gone wrong, the day was much calmer than Lynn anticipated. She received two panicked messages from the secretary but was able to handle the problems in a matter of minutes. At Bryan's insistence, a couple of high-school students had been called into service to handle some of the more routine details, which meant that the men employed by Stone Stock could concentrate on preparation for the evening's events. Lynn found time to bring the Stone books up-to-date, pay an outstanding feed bill and advance two of the drivers a little much-needed money.

Lynn heard that the rodeo clown who'd been dismissed was hanging around. When she mentioned that to Bryan, he went in search of Tate but reported back that the man hadn't had anything new to say.

"I hate to see his problems with a bottle get the best of him. I hope he'll find AA one day, but only he can make that decision," Bryan said.

It wasn't until she was waiting her turn to compete that Lynn admitted how much she'd needed to feel her strong, well-trained horse under her and to be facing a challenge that she knew how to handle. "We're going to do it tonight, old girl," she told the excited mare. "You and I, we understand each other. We think alike." Lynn turned pensive. "Maybe you're the only one who does understand me."

That night cowgirl and horse were in perfect harmony. White Moon was eager to run and wanted nothing more than to please her owner.

For her part, Lynn wiped everything but the run from her mind. She existed for one reason; to guide White Moon with love and body language. Even after the last barrel had been mastered and the finish line was only a few pounding hoofbeats away, Lynn didn't resort to the riding crop. White Moon needed no encouragement. She was racing for herself, for Lynn, for the courage in her heart.

Lynn straightened and reached for the sky as soon as she crossed the finish line. She didn't need to hear her time announced to know that she and White Moon had completed a spectacular ride. Under seventeen seconds! First place, easy!

"Yes, my lady!" Lynn laughed, leaning over White Moon's sweating neck, "You did it, White Moon! We did it! I love you!"

Suddenly Bryan was beside her. She looked down, barely recognizing him in the quiet, shadowed place where White Moon had stopped. "Good ride," he told her, his voice soft in contrast to Lynn's excited tones.

"It felt good, Bryan. I've needed to feel like this for so long. I'm happy tonight. Really happy."

Was it only the night, or was Bryan creating his own shadows? "It isn't official yet," he was telling her. "But you may have broken the record here."

"I did?" Lynn knew her time was extraordinary, but to break a record was almost beyond her comprehension. A joyous smile broke free. "I've waited so long for it to be right. And I was right."

"About what?"

"About competing again." Lynn straightened and hugged herself. "I missed the feeling so much. I feel like—I feel like I'm back in touch with myself."

Bryan let her go then. White Moon needed to have her saddle removed and Bryan had to get back in the ring, but he took with him the frightening echo of Lynn's words. It was as he'd believed; competing was what she'd been looking for.

The thought of that depressed Bryan for the rest of the evening. Occasionally he spotted Lynn among the cowboys and cowgirls. It seemed that someone was always congratulating her. Even from a distance, he could feel pride radiating from her.

Bryan was certain that she'd never smiled or laughed like that when they were together.

It was past midnight when Lynn finally wound down enough that she thought she would be able to sleep. She'd taken White Moon to the corral hours before but she wanted to check in on her one last time before seeking her own bed.

White Moon wasn't there.

Confused, Lynn opened the corral gate and stepped inside. A half dozen quarter horses were dozing, but there was no sign of the mare who had performed so magnificently. Thoroughly alarmed, Lynn searched for the wranglers, hoping against hope that one of them had moved her.

They hadn't. "We wouldn't touch that mare of yours without asking, Lynn." One of the older hands lifted his head off his pillow in the barn where he and many of the hands were spending the night. "You're sure the gate was locked? None of the other horses is missing?"

Lynn shook her head. "I'm always so careful with her. I know I was excited tonight, but there's no way I'd—"

"Hey. Settle down now." Pete climbed out from under his sleeping bag. He kicked at the man next to him. "We'll find her."

Pete was wrong. Although a half dozen men spent the next several hours combing the grounds looking for White Moon, there was no sign of the mare. Even when Bryan took charge, Lynn was unable to still the fear that was crawling through her. White Moon was worth thousands of dollars; more than that, she held a special place in Lynn's heart. A dozen illogical possibilities occurred to her. Some other cowgirl had stolen the valuable horse. Someone, maybe she, hadn't secured the gate and White Moon had slipped out.

"I can't think," Lynn moaned as it began to get light. "What if she's scared, maybe hurt? Bryan? What if I never see her again?"

Bryan wasn't going to try to pass off Lynn's concern. "Then you'll have to learn to live without her, Lynn. I'm sorry. I'm so sorry."

Lynn clung to Bryan. "If it's my fault—I know. There's nothing you or anyone else can say. She's just the most important thing in my life right now."

Bryan tried to talk Lynn into getting something to eat, but Lynn was too upset. As much as she needed him to keep her from unraveling, she had to let him go. "I'll keep on looking," she told him with her arms wrapped tightly around her unsettled stomach. "You have other things you have to do."

"I'll be back as soon as I can," Bryan said. His eyes were somber, his voice deep and quiet.

Five hours later Lynn had given up all hope. She sat slumped in the grounds office trying to work up an ad to place in the local newspaper. Bryan had come by numerous times. Although he hadn't been able to give her news of White Moon, Lynn was grateful for his presence. Now, when her hand trembled, Bryan took over the chore. "We'll use the home phone of one of the committee members. That way there'll be a local number for people to call."

But will anyone call? Lynn wanted to ask. She didn't; there was no way Bryan could answer that question. She was trying to decide what to say about a reward when the phone rang. After a minute, the secretary turned it over to Lynn. "Maybe," she whispered. "Someone's reporting a horse that showed up on a school playground."

Lynn grabbed the phone. "I didn't know who else to call," the woman on the other end of the line was saying. "I guess I could have called the police or animal control, but they probably wouldn't know what to do with it any more than I did. She's such a beautiful creature. So gentle. She seems kind of confused, though."

Lynn quickly described White Moon. A moment later she gave Bryan a smile that was a heartbeat away from tears. "They've found her," she mouthed. "Thank God, they've found her." After taking down the school's address and hanging up, Lynn continued. "The school's about five miles away. Bryan? How did she get there?"

Bryan was already reaching for truck keys. "We'll probably never know, Lynn," he told her as he opened the door. "I'm just glad we got her back."

"Me, too." Lynn blinked. She couldn't stop the tears; she wasn't even trying. "I'm so glad we got her back."

"Because she's everything to you," Bryan said so softly that Lynn didn't hear.

IN FIVE DAYS Stone Stock would be back in Harney county. Meanwhile, Lynn and Bryan continued to sleep together. Their lovemaking left them shaken with its intensity. Each night Lynn would come to the trailer wondering whether last night's perfection had been a fluke. Surely there was a limit to how much pleasure they could give each other. But every time they came together, the current was stronger, the waves more intense.

There was only one flaw—they didn't talk. Whenever Lynn tried to, Bryan remained silent.

Lynn saw the coming time back at home as a respite. Despite the constant traveling, her continuing success in her event, work, and all the people around them, she felt as if she and Bryan had been locked together too long. They needed time apart. At least she did. Maybe before they hit the road again, Lynn would understand where, if anywhere, their lovemaking was headed.

At home, she was relieved to find Bullet not only up and around but chafing at his enforced inactivity. He trailed after his older brother, questioning Chet's management of the ranch and prompting his usually mellow brother to demand that he mind his own business. Bullet tried to help in the kitchen until his mother threatened to lock him in the barn. The only ones who were happy to have Bullet underfoot were his niece and nephews.

Lynn decided that the accident hadn't changed Bullet. He was still restless, driven, goal oriented. What was driving him crazy was that, until he'd been given the green light from the doctor, he couldn't pursue his goal.

"It's awfully hard on him," Dee told Lynn when the two women were able to grab a few minutes alone. "He isn't used to having a short rope thrown over him."

Lynn laughed at the picture Dee had painted, but she was determined to make the most of their privacy. She told Dee that Bullet, as she'd expected, had made light of the doctor's cautions. Was Bullet really healing as well as he said he was?

"He is," Dee said softly. "I know him too well for him to get away with anything."

Dee's tone stopped Lynn. She'd been watching a lizard climbing a fence post, but now she turned toward her friend. Something was in Dee's eyes that hadn't been there before. Dee was softer. There was no other way Lynn could describe what she found. "Tell me about it."

"About how Bullet's doing?"

"About how you feel."

It was Dee's turn to focus on the lizard. "Am I that transparent?"

"I'm afraid so, my friend. Bullet isn't the bratty kid next door anymore, is he?"

Dee shook her head. But her tone said everything. "I don't know what he is anymore, Lynn. I don't... He'd been on my mind a lot before the accident. I guess you know that. He and I have been together almost constantly since I got to Dallas. I held his hand in the hospital. He smiled at me even when I don't think he knew where he was. We fought together to get him back home. Since then we've gone for long walks and talked. There's so much more to him than I ever knew before."

"And you like what you're learning."

"How did you guess?"

Lynn could have told Dee that she was aware of what was in Dee's heart because hers was on the same path, but this conversation was about Dee and Bullet, not Lynn and Bryan. "It's in your eyes," she said instead. "Are you in love with him?"

"Love? What a scary word! I don't know. Your brother has set goals for himself. I haven't known

enough men, outside my brother, who are like that."
Dee looked up at Lynn. "Yes. I guess I am."

Dee and Bullet. Lynn was trying to keep pace, but
this was all too much. "Does he know it?"

"I think so. We . . . well, because of his injuries, all
we've done is talk and hold hands, and kiss." Dee
didn't blush. "I know he'd like more than that. But I
think he's just as confused as I am over what's happening."

"Have the two of you talked about that?"

Dee shook her head. "What we talk about is his
frustration. How much he has invested in rodeoing.
How he has to get back on the circuit. He's so single-
minded, Lynn."

Because she'd known Dee forever, Lynn recognized
the quiet desperation in her voice. Dee might be in
love, but this was no fairy-tale love. She'd given her
heart to a man who put the pursuit of his goal before
everything else, even the woman in his life. Lynn
wanted to shake Bullet, to make him understand that
he might never reach the goal he'd set, and meanwhile he risked losing something much more precious.

But Lynn couldn't make Bullet's decisions for him.
"He is single-minded," Lynn agreed. "And stubborn
and bullheaded and impulsive and a thousand other
things only his sister can get away with saying."

For the first time since they began speaking, Dee
laughed. "Not anymore, my friend. I've pointed those
same things out to him myself."

"And he hasn't told you to take a flying leap?"

"That's the amazing thing. He sits there and nods
his head and agrees with me and then does what he
was going to do, anyway."

"He loves you."

Dee's eyes glistened. "Do you think so."

"I know so. I know that bullheaded brother of mine. If someone's opinion wasn't important to him, he wouldn't sit around long enough to hear it."

Dee looked as if she was going to say something. Instead she nodded slowly, blinking until the telltale light was out of her eyes. "We aren't going to resolve anything overnight. Bullet and I have a long way to go. Maybe something will come out of it and maybe... But then, I'm not the only one who's trying to figure out a man, am I?"

Lynn started at the sudden turn in the conversation, but she'd known it was coming. "Maybe."

"Maybe nothing. Don't forget, I was on hand when Bryan walked out of that trailer one morning."

Lynn felt no need to deny Dee's honesty. This was her best friend, her lover's sister. Dee had just exposed her own heart. Lynn couldn't do any less. "I haven't been able to figure Bryan out. I think that's asking the impossible. However, I have learned one thing. Bryan isn't the distant creature I once thought he was."

"I told you that." Dee picked up a stick and held it in front of the lizard. The tiny reptile crawled over it without breaking stride. "Has he recovered? I mean, is Heather behind him?"

It was Lynn's turn to place something in front of the tireless lizard. She selected a dry leaf. It was less of an obstacle than the stick. "We haven't talked about that for a long time."

"What have you talked about?"

Dee had asked an unbelievably hard question. Lynn wasn't happy with the answer she had to give. "Work. Having to dismiss a clown."

Dee obviously wasn't buying Lynn's explanation. "That's what you talk about when you're... together?"

"No, that isn't what we talk about," she finally admitted. "The truth is we don't do much talking."

"Is that good or bad?"

"I don't know," Lynn groaned. "I think it's safer if we leave certain subjects alone."

"And I think that's asking for trouble."

"What choice do I have, Dee? I can't force him to talk."

"He doesn't tell you what he's thinking?"

"No. And, I don't tell him what I'm thinking."

"What *is* on your mind?"

For an instant, Lynn drew a blank. When Bryan touched her, she was aware of nothing except their sharing. But before and after they'd made love she thought. Too much. Thoughts that were all questions and no answers. "I love him, Dee."

Dee blinked. "Just like that? No question about it?"

"No question."

"Then why don't you tell him?"

"I'm..." Lynn took a deep breath. "I think I'm afraid."

It wouldn't have surprised Lynn to have Dee laugh at her insane words. Instead Dee pulled her close for a quick hug. "Of what?"

"Of..." Once again Lynn had to struggle before she could give the words freedom. "I think maybe I'm afraid of exposing too much of myself. Dee, what if he doesn't feel the same way?"

"You'll never know unless you ask him."

"I know that!" Lynn snapped and then relented. "Dee, his answer is so important. What if he doesn't love me?"

"I don't believe that for a moment. You know what I think? I think each of you is waiting for the other one to start talking. Talk about clouding up an issue. Why don't you take the plunge?"

"Because he's married to that damn business of his. It claims so much of him."

"Don't I know it," Dee answered softly.

Lynn nodded. Dee had released her, but the memory of her touch continued to give Lynn courage. "Dee, I've watched him put in twenty-hour days. I've seen him risk injury and never give it a thought. I know how much he believes in what he's doing. I think he gets back as much as he gives out. Rodeoing—that's his life."

"If it is, then it's a darn poor excuse for a life."

Dee was right, of course, but neither of them could control the flow of Bryan Stone's existence. Lynn had only herself to offer. And she didn't feel she could point to her own life with the same kind of pride Bryan had a right to. She rode a horse. She didn't run a business that helped hundreds of people earn a living and brought pleasure to thousands.

"I wouldn't try to change him, Dee," Lynn told Bryan's sister. "Even if I could, I wouldn't try. I don't think he'd be the man I love if I did."

"Are you saying you don't believe Bryan has enough room in his heart for both you and his lifestyle?"

Dee had found the core of Lynn's fear. It was as simple as that. "I don't know. I'm afraid to ask."

MEMORIES OF THAT CONVERSATION stayed with Lynn for the rest of the day and into the evening, when Dee insisted on having the whole Walker clan over for dinner. Lynn tried to distract herself by concentrating on her family and lending Dee a hand, but her mind kept coming back to Dee's question. There was no denying that what he did for a living commanded a great deal of Bryan's dedication.

Maybe there wasn't enough left over for her. As long as they were traveling together they would take and receive pleasure from each other. But what if Lynn took herself out of Bryan's presence? Would he ask her to come back or would responsibilities and commitments wash over him like the tide washes over a beach; sweeping his memory of her out to sea?

This was driving her crazy! In saner moments, Lynn realized that she might be worrying about pitfalls and heartache that simply didn't exist. She reminded herself that the right questions might result in the right answers. But how to ask those questions, and how to go on if his response wasn't what she longed to hear?

Lynn needed to be alone. After dinner, Lynn quietly excused herself. Chet and his family had already left with Carol. Bullet had told his mother that Lynn would give him a lift later. Then both he and Dee had disappeared. Bryan had closed himself in his office.

Lynn took refuge outside, walking in the hot wind blowing in from the distant mountains. She wandered without thinking, absorbing sights and smells, returning to her childhood.

It was beautiful out here. The scent of sage was in her nostrils. The call of a lonely owl was the only assault on the prairie silence and that sound belonged there. Many people would have felt uneasy in the middle of all this vastness, but Lynn had felt its pulse since infancy.

A person could think out here. A woman could listen to her heart.

She had left the compound composed of ranch house, outbuildings and barns, and followed a shadowed fence line until she was no longer distracted by the light burning outside the main barn. She'd come to love the hectic pace of the rodeos. Even now she could remember its exciting sounds and scents.

Ranch and rodeo grounds, Lynn thought. They each had a place in her heart. But tonight all she wanted was to be alone. To let her thoughts flow free and maybe, somehow, collect themselves.

"Lynn?"

There was only one voice with the power to reach that deeply into her. Lynn turned and waited for Bryan to join her. They stood side by side, silent, not touching. It didn't matter. Lynn felt touched.

"Did you talk to Dee?"

Lynn nodded. "I think she's the best medicine my brother could have. Have you talked to him?"

"Only enough to know he's not going to stay here much longer."

"Why doesn't that news surprise me?" Lynn searched her mind for a way to keep the conversation going, but they'd exhausted the one topic that came easily to both of them. She could have continued on her aimless exploration of the fence line, but, with Bryan there, it no longer seemed important.

Bryan looked up, concentrating on the moon. "It's quiet out here."

"Do you miss the noise?"

"Not really. I like the activity and I like the quiet. They balance each other out."

Lynn agreed. She didn't think she could take the hectic pace of a rodeo constantly, but neither could she spend her life cut off entirely from the world beyond the ranch. Peace, she believed, came not from where she was, but who she was with. "Mom's looking good. I think she's put on a little weight."

"I noticed that. There was a letter from my folks."

So there were still other things they could talk about, after all. Holding that thought to her, Lynn asked about Bryan's parents. They were now on their way to Mexico for no better reason than the fact that they had never been there before. "Dad wants to see a bullfight. Mom says if he goes to one, he's going without her."

"It sounds as if they're having a wonderful time."

"They are." Bryan's sigh was so soft that only someone attuned to him would have heard it. "I envy them."

"What? Their freedom?"

"I'm glad they have each other to share this time in their lives."

Lynn didn't try to speak. Bryan had been able to read a chatty letter and sense what was important, below the surface. She reached for his hand. Hand in hand they watched the moon for several minutes.

Bryan broke the silence. "We're going to have to leave tomorrow. At least I am. Do you still want to go?"

Do you want me? "I— Why shouldn't I?"

"I thought maybe you'd want to spend more time with your family. Do you?" That wasn't why he'd asked the question at all. Bryan remembered what Lynn had been like when she'd broken the rodeo record. If that emotion still claimed her, nothing could have kept her from hitting the road again with White Moon. He didn't know what place, if any, he had in her future, but he'd had to ask his questions.

They weren't the questions Lynn wanted to hear. What her heart needed was to know whether her presence made any difference in Bryan's life. "No," she told him. "It looks as if they've been able to muddle along without me."

Lynn sensed that Bryan was nodding. He was still holding her hand, but she wasn't sure he was aware of it. "I'm grateful to you," she told him. "I would never have been able to compete if it hadn't been for you."

"I'm glad I could do it for you."

This was insane! They'd lain in each others arms, heard the beating of each other's hearts. There were things they needed to talk about. Lynn had to ask. "What's going to happen tomorrow?"

"What do you mean?" His hand tightened around hers.

"I mean . . . with us." This was so hard! "Are we going to go on the way we have been?"

"Do you want to?"

Why should he be the one to ask all the questions? "I think you know the answer to that, Bryan. I— you're important to me. I need what we've started."

Lynn was aware of the shudder that charged through Bryan, and she felt the same way. "What have we started, Lynn?" he asked.

Love. Love has started. The emotion floated high and free before Lynn could bury it deep and safe again inside her. She found the strength to speak. "I've fallen in love with you."

"You . . . Lynn." His grip tightened. He opened his mouth but said nothing more.

"But don't worry," Lynn heard herself say when his silence became too much to bear. She felt naked and exposed and terribly lonely. "It isn't serious. Nothing you need to worry about."

"Nothing I need to worry about?" His whisper barely reached her.

"Nothing that will get in the way of what I want to do." Lynn felt empty. She'd opened herself to him and he hadn't responded. There was only one thing she could do. Lynn pulled her hand free and started to retrace her steps. She thought she could hear Bryan's quick breath behind her but she couldn't be sure. She didn't dare ask.

And wouldn't look back. ——————

Chapter Eleven

The California Rodeo was first held in Salinas in 1911. It was now one of the largest in the nation. As a consequence, Stone Stock had pulled out all the stops in order to have top-notch broncs and bulls on hand for it. Lynn was pleased that Red, despite his rocky start, had turned into a flashy, consistent bucker who had earned his place in the first string.

Cowboys who entered four or five rodeos a week saw Salinas as a place where they would be assured of a professionally run show. As independent men in a dependent world, they had respect for the support staff that held them in high regard. To the California Rodeo organizers, cowboys were more than drawing cards. The men and women behind that rodeo understood that without cowboys, they would have nothing.

Bryan understood that also. That was why he'd come a day early and insisted on having each and every one of his bucking stock checked by the local vets. Hearing that Jagger Duncan had found another clown to work with him and they were already on the grounds also relieved his mind. Focusing on the job helped keep his mind occupied. He had no such refuge for his heart.

Lynn, too, was looking for diversion. Since that night at the ranch, she'd felt half alive. She'd given Bryan so much, and yet she now felt they'd shared nothing. He didn't need her love. Lynn wasn't sure she could survive that. The silence between them was slowly eating away at her. They'd gone to Laramie, Wyoming, and Branson, Montana, where she'd devoted herself to White Moon and they'd had two more first-place finishes.

That was what felt good about her world. Bryan had gone back to sleeping in his foreman's trailer.

Lynn was too proud to ask what had gone wrong, and Bryan offered no explanation. She could travel in a different truck, cling to Dee's side, busy herself with mind-dulling chores. She could tell herself that competing was the only goal she needed. What she couldn't do was look at Bryan and not remember their nights together, and wonder how she could have been so wrong about him.

It might have been easier if she could talk to Dee about it, but the cowgirl had become just as silent as her brother. Lynn understood that Dee was concerned about Bullet, who was still at the ranch, but it wasn't like Dee to stay down emotionally for more than a day. At her suggestion, Dee had called home, but Lynn had had to drag the results of that phone call out of Dee.

"All right, I guess," Dee said in response to Lynn's question about how Bullet was doing. "He's leaving for Colorado today."

"Colorado? What's there?"

"Some rodeo in Craig. Bullet says it's time for him to get back to work. He just doesn't want to jump off the deep end. That's why he's starting small."

"That's good, I guess." Lynn frowned. Dee looked worried and that frightened her. "What's wrong?"

"Nothing." Dee was looking everywhere but at Lynn. "He... If he does all right in Craig, he's going to give Cheyenne a try next week."

Lynn whistled. The Cheyenne Frontier Days were big time. If he went there, Bullet would be competing against the best in the business, including many who were now in Salinas. Bryan had hoped to be able to take his stock to Cheyenne, but because the two rodeos fell so close together this year, he'd had to decide between them. "Is that all he had to say?" Lynn probed gently. "Does he have any idea when you're going to see each other again?"

It was the right question, but for a moment, Lynn was sorry she'd asked. The tears she'd already heard in her friend's voice were now released. Angrily Dee swiped them away. "Probably never if Bullet has his way."

Impulsively, Lynn wrapped her arms around Dee, waiting for her friend to give her emotions full expression. Dee struggled for control, and once that control came, she stood straight, her fingers laced tightly together. "He's so stubborn," Dee started. She took a shuddering breath and went on. "You know how he is about this rodeoing business. It's his life. I swear it's the only goal he has."

"It has been for years. The accident didn't change anything."

"I wondered. I thought maybe... I should have known it wouldn't." Dee had been staring at her trembling hands, but now she bravely raised her eyes so Lynn could see her pain. "Bullet—I asked if he wanted me with him."

"You did?" Lynn asked softly.

"I had to. I needed to hear his answer." Dee stopped. Her chin trembled, and she blinked rapidly, but she didn't cry.

"What did he tell you? I'm sorry," Lynn relented. "I know it's none of my business, but I think you need to talk about it."

"I do. Lynn, he didn't want me."

"No! That fool. He doesn't have the brains he was born with."

"Don't." Dee stopped Lynn's tirade. "You don't know everything. It isn't what you think. He cares for me." Dee brightened softly. "I know he does."

"Then why doesn't he want to see you?"

"Because I think he's afraid I'll come between him and his goal."

"He's afraid of that?" Lynn was glad Bullet wasn't there right now. If she could get her hands on him and give him a piece of her mind about putting people who cared for him through misery, he'd be sorry he'd ever been born. Bullet might be her brother, but Dee was her best friend. Lynn knew the pain that went with not knowing where she stood with the man she loved. She understood, firsthand, what Dee was going through. "That's the craziest thing I've ever heard of."

"Is it?" Dee managed. "Do you know what he told me? The day he got hurt, he was thinking of me. He didn't have his mind on what he was doing."

"And he's blaming you for that? Dee? He can't be blaming you for his accident. If anything, he should take it as proof that there's more to life than trying to get rich.''

"It isn't just the money." Dee sounded as if she wasn't sure of anything. "Lynn, he doesn't have many years left in the business. You know that. If all those years of sacrifice are going to bear fruit, it has to be now."

"Then he'll wind up famous and alone. What kind of a life is that?"

"Bullet doesn't see it that way. He's . . . Making it to the top has been on his mind for so long he can't look at anything else. At least he has a goal..." Dee's voice trailed off and Lynn barely heard the last words.

"What are you saying?" Lynn prompted. "That you don't have a goal? What about the business?"

"The only thing I want out of life now is Bullet. Only he has reservations about our being together. I understand. Believe me, I understand. If I distracted him, if he failed because of me, I'd hate myself. But if I stay here, what does that leave me with?"

Dee sounded so desperate and alone that her pain tore through Lynn. Once again she put her arms around Dee. This time her friend didn't pull away. Dee wasn't crying, but Lynn felt the battle not to. "I don't know what that leaves you with," Lynn said with an honesty she knew would hurt both of them. "I wish I had some answers, but I don't." How can I, Lynn asked herself. I don't have any answers for myself.

Dee was silent for the better part of a minute. Lynn sensed her inner struggle. The time Dee had had with Bullet in Dallas and later back at the ranch had accomplished nothing except to cement Dee's love for the young cowboy. But those days had been days apart from the reality of both their lives.

Lynn still wanted to shake Bullet. Dee Stone was a good woman, maybe the only one who could truly understand him. Bullet might believe he could put her on hold until he'd reached his goal, but Dee wasn't an inanimate object. She was a passionate, loving woman and she wanted to share her passion and love with Bullet. If Bullet couldn't recognize that, he was going to lose her.

"I'll live," Dee said shakily. "I don't have much choice."

"I know that. But you must feel as if you've lost something you'll never get back."

Dee nodded. "That's what makes it so hard. But, Lynn, I love Bullet. Part of loving someone else is allowing them to live their own lives. If this is what Bullet needs to do at this point in his life, I'm not going to stand in his way."

"Do you really think your being with him would jeopardize his future?"

"That's for Bullet to decide. What I do know is, I'm not going to be the one to turn him from his goal."

"What about your goals? Your life?"

Dee laughed bitterly, sorrow showing through. "I can't answer that now, Lynn. All I know is, I have to let Bullet go. If I didn't, one day he'd hate me."

Lynn went through the rest of the day feeling as if her own emotions had been exposed as much as her friend's as a result of their conversation. They'd been talking about Dee's romance, but there were too many similarities. Physical distance separated Dee and Bullet. But the emotional distance between Lynn and Bryan was just as real, just as powerful.

BRYAN HAD SEEN THE TWO WOMEN talking and wondered if he was being discussed, or if their conversation had been about Lynn's spectacular rides over the past few days. He'd tried to lose himself in his work since they left home, pushing himself until his body cried out for rest. Maybe if he was able to sleep, he wouldn't think about how quickly Lynn had carved a place for herself among the barrel racing elite. If she continued at her present pace, she would make more money this year than she had in the past three. Not only that, but Lynn Walker was a natural for the boot, saddle and hat companies that were always looking for attractive, confident women to promote their products.

When that happened, Lynn would have found what Bryan believed she was looking for. She'd have her own horse trailer, maybe more than one horse, and a place as one of those at the top of the rodeo competitors' world. Bryan would no longer be able to look up from his work and find her beside him.

His heart had done a quick, quiet dance when she'd told him she loved him, but the dance had stopped with her next words. It seemed that love, for Lynn, had no more substance than the wind. "Don't worry," she'd told him. "It isn't serious." Then she'd gone on to tell him he didn't have to worry. She wasn't asking anything of him in return.

Bryan had worked to give a great deal of himself that night. If she hadn't tossed off her love, if she hadn't established its narrow boundaries, she would now be holding his heart. But she'd thrown up barriers, and let Bryan know that he wasn't to come any closer.

That was why Bryan was sleeping in Randy Steller's trailer.

Bryan waited until Dee had left before walking over to the holding pen where Lynn was standing. The pen was empty; there was no reason for him to be there, but he came, anyway.

Lynn looked up as he approached, but she didn't say anything to him. The burden was on him. "Is she all right?" he asked. "Dee's been pretty quiet lately."

"We've all been pretty quiet," Lynn said so softly she wasn't sure Bryan could hear her. "She's been talking to Bullet. That has her down." Lynn wanted to press past the barriers between them. Maybe talking about emotion, even someone else's emotions, would chip away at the walls. "Bullet's back on the circuit. He's going to compete tomorrow."

"I'd think that would please my sister. She wants him back on his feet."

"That she does. However, my dumb brother doesn't want her with him."

Bryan frowned. "What did Bullet say?" he asked.

"That he's bullheaded and single-minded and has his nose to the wind. No," Lynn corrected himself. "It's a lot more complicated than that."

Brother and sister were a great deal alike. Having a goal was paramount with them. "Bullet's after something not many people can accomplish," he told Lynn. "He's making it because the only thing he sees is his goal."

"I know that."

"He has to have a target, Lynn." Bryan hated the words he was saying.

"I know that, Bryan. Remember, I'm his sister. But does having a target mean he has to be alone?"

Lynn's question stopped Bryan. She was talking about herself as much as about her brother. He wanted nothing more than to hear that she wasn't as single-minded as Bullet. "Bullet was injured once," he said. "He's risking aggravating that injury or getting another one, but that isn't stopping him. He has something to prove to himself. Dee has to understand that."

"You think she doesn't?"

Bryan steeled himself to weather her anger. He'd walked over here hoping to cut away at the distance that had grown between them. He didn't feel he was succeeding, but any words, no matter what the outcome, had to be better than silence between them. "Dee has to share Bullet's commitment. Until she can do that, there isn't enough to hold them together."

"Dee has to share Bullet's commitment." Lynn turned Bryan's words around, finding wisdom in them. Bryan would never expect a woman to sacrifice herself for a man. But, somehow, their two very different minds and hearts had to find a common ground.

And not just Dee and Bullet, Lynn understood. A barrier stood between her and Bryan. Neither of them knew how to tear it down. "There aren't any easy answers in life, are there?" she said.

"Not for the important questions."

Bryan could be incredibly perceptive when it came to the human mind. Unfortunately his heart was another story. Lynn let her eyes slide to Bryan's bare chest. There, beneath tanned flesh, muscle and bone, lay his heart. Maybe it was open to receive her love; maybe it wasn't. Lynn didn't know the answer to that. The only thing she knew was that if she stood out here with Bryan much longer, he'd know how lonely her nights had been.

How much she needed him. It was not his love-making that she needed, but his love. She wouldn't take one without the other.

"I have to go. It's time to exercise White Moon."

"White Moon? Yeah. White Moon. Lynn, I wish you the best tonight."

"Thank you," Lynn managed to say through her pain. "I'm going to have a lot of competition. I need to be ready."

"You will be. You and White Moon, there's something very special between the two of you."

Don't say that, Bryan, Lynn thought as she turned away. She didn't want him to be so understanding of her, to make her believe he was thinking about more than the few nights they'd shared. If he said anything, if he said the right things, her heart would soar. And the crash when it came might very well kill her.

BRYAN HAD BEEN RIGHT. There was something between Lynn and White Moon that evening that came close to being magical. White Moon's smooth rhythm turned a fiery performance into a thing of grace and beauty that brought the audience to its feet. Lynn had dressed in white and her pale hair streamed free behind her as she lifted her hat to acknowledge the applause.

For a few seconds she was able to forget that barrel racing was no longer, if it had ever been, the only thing she wanted out of life.

Mounted on his stallion, Bryan watched. Others might have seen the perfect union between horse and rider, but Bryan saw only the slender young woman.

He thought he could be detached, that he would be able to see nothing more than an athlete when he looked at Lynn. But then his heart came undone. Her eyes, he believed, were alive with nothing more than the joy of accomplishment.

There was no fear in her. Lynn could lean with her mare, her feet inches from the ground; her perch in the saddle assured only as long as White Moon didn't stumble. Bryan had watched her brother ride broncs no sane man would attempt to mount; his sister had the same guts. The same raw determination.

He wanted her. Wanted her body and mind, but most of all, Bryan wanted Lynn's heart. He would give up everything for that. But the hell of it was, her heart wasn't his to take. "It isn't serious. Nothing you need to worry about," she'd said.

What would her answer be tonight if he asked whether her love had grown or diminished. Bryan was afraid he knew the answer. "What love?" she would ask him.

He should have said something that night at the ranch. He should have told her he understood because he, too, was in love. Only with him, it was a serious case.

He hadn't spoken. And the magical moment had been lost.

THE NEXT MORNING, reporters from a local newspaper and two TV stations descended on the rodeo. Bryan was asked what seemed like hundreds of questions. Although he did his best to come up with fresh answers, his heart wasn't in it. Lynn was asked to put her white costume back on and mount White Moon for the cameras. Bryan watched. He was so damn proud of her that he could hardly contain the emotion, and yet seeing her in the spotlight brought back a painful reminder of what separated them.

He wasn't given much time to think about those emotions. He was still within listening distance of the interviewers when the president of the rodeo committee approached him. "Bryan. We have to talk."

"Problems?"

"Major. In private, please."

BRYAN WASN'T AROUND when Lynn returned White Moon to the corral. A couple of cowgirls dropped by to tease Lynn about the attention she was getting, but they didn't stay long. Foremost on Lynn's mind was getting out of her dressy outfit. She barely took note of the tall man coming toward her.

"Lynn? Do you have a minute?"

Tate. Lynn hadn't seen or heard about the clown since Bryan had let him go. "I guess so. What have you been up to?"

Tate's smile reminded Lynn of how young he was. "Good things. I've been at a treatment center. For my drinking. I was just thinking, well, I was hoping maybe you'd tell Bryan that. I've got a handle on it now; I really do. I'm not sure he wants anything to do with me and, well, the truth of it is, I'm not sure what I'd say to him."

"You aren't drinking anymore? Tate, that's wonderful."

"I think it is." Tate hooked his hands in his rear pockets. "You wouldn't mind telling Bryan that, would you? Let him know I checked myself into that place for a couple of weeks. Now I'm going to meetings. You wouldn't believe the number of meetings

I'm going to. I'm in town to see a couple of friends. I thought I'd drop by and take in the rodeo. I guess once it's in your blood, there's no getting rid of it. I was here last night. Your ride—it was really something.''

"Thank you." Talking to Tate was easier than she'd thought it would be. If Tate wanted to talk about his drinking, she would encourage him. "Are you sure you don't want to see Bryan? I know he'd like to hear about it."

"I'm not so sure about that." Tate glanced around. "He was pretty disappointed in me. There's a lot about that period I don't remember, but I do remember Bryan being disappointed in me."

Lynn couldn't deny that. "As long as you have your problem under control, that's the main thing. You don't have to hurry off, do you? I'm not sure what Bryan's up to, but maybe he'd have a minute to talk to you."

"No. No." Tate pulled his hands out of his pocket. "Maybe—" He smiled. "Give me a little more time. Maybe after I've been dry longer. I mean it, that ride of yours was something."

"I can't take all the credit. I have a special horse."

"White Moon. Yeah, she's good all right. She means the world to you, doesn't she?"

"Just about. The right horse makes all the difference."

"Yeah. I'm just glad you found her that time. Did you ever figure out how she got out?"

Lynn shook her head. "It was a long time before I let her out of my sight after that. Those hours of not knowing whether I'd ever see her again— Even now I don't want to think about it."

"I don't blame you." Tate glanced around again. "You haven't seen Jagger have you? I'd kind of like to say hello. Look, I'm not going to take up any more of your time. Just tell Bryan what I said, will you? Maybe in a few more months, he'll consider giving me another chance. And keep White Moon away from school grounds."

It took Lynn only a few minutes to change clothes. She wanted to tell Bryan that Tate had taken control of his life, but it took quite a while for Lynn to find Bryan, and when she did, he had no time for her. He was in an emergency meeting with the entire membership of the Salinas rodeo steering committee.

No one was sure what the meeting was about, but speculation ran rampant. Several humane society officials had been poking around the stock earlier that day. Then the rodeo committee was asked to meet with them. Now Bryan and Dee had been called in. Lynn paced restlessly for the better part of an hour, her agitation growing with every minute. This was no casual meeting to tie up loose ends before tonight's performance.

At last Dee emerged from the rodeo grounds office. After a quick glance at Dee's somber features, Lynn's worst fears were confirmed. The two women exchanged glances, but Lynn knew better than to say anything until they were alone.

"It's all a pack of lies," Dee hissed once the two women were alone in their trailer. She folded her arms, her fingers tightly gripping her flesh. "But the committee's so stirred up they won't listen."

"What's a pack of lies?" Lynn pressed. "I have no idea what you're talking about."

"Neither do the humane officials. They're so suspicious. How they get off accusing us of feeding our stock spoiled hay... And that business about packing them in like sardines while we're traveling. You know that isn't true."

"Of course I do." Dee's anger and frustration was infectious. "Who's saying this?"

"They say that's confidential. Confidential! How are we going to defend ourselves if we don't know where the accusations are coming from? Lynn, you know that some of the people who handle the stock aren't the world's most dependable. Getting people who are willing to travel, well, you know what that's like. I feel better when we hire college students, but that isn't always possible. We had to let two men go just last week because they weren't dependable. If this is their way of getting even... There's even supposed to be pictures."

"Wait a minute," Lynn tried to slow her friend down. "You're making it sound like a trial."

"It is, almost. Where could pictures have come from? How come we can't see them? I don't know how Bryan can stay so calm. I know I'd like to punch someone's lights out. The idea that we'd do anything to hurt the stock—"

Lynn could imagine Dee popping someone in the nose. Few things brought out such passion in Dee Stone. Lately, one was Bullet Walker. Another was the family business. "Don't you have a right to see the evidence?"

"That's what Bryan keeps telling them. I like to think he's getting that point through their thick skulls, but you can't believe the damage there'll be to our reputation if this isn't resolved pretty soon. This is the

second time we've been put through this this year.
Yeah, I know, there wasn't much to that business in
Union, but this... This is making us sound like Jack
the Ripper." Dee landed heavily on her bed. "The rodeo committee doesn't want to believe the charges, of
course, but the way they're looking at us... I know
what they're thinking. Where there's smoke, there's
fire."

"They're just being cautious," Lynn tried to point
out. It wasn't going to do any good if Dee got so upset that she couldn't think straight. "They don't like
being caught in the middle."

"Who cares about them! It's our reputation that's
on the line. Where's Bryan? He said he was going to
be right out."

Lynn tensed as the trailer door opened, but when
Bryan stepped inside she managed to relax a little and
concentrate again on their problems. Bryan's mind
would be on the charges, not her. "Dee told me," she
said. "What happens now?"

Bryan turned toward Lynn. Although sunlight was
coming through the small windows, Lynn was unable
to gauge his mood. It seemed that he stared at her
forever before answering her question, but maybe it
was only her reaction to him that made time slow
down. "What happens is that we're kept dangling
while the humane people keep on looking. They're
questioning everyone. Drivers, stock handlers, even
some guy who hasn't been on the payroll for months.
I have no idea how they got a hold of him."

"How long is that all going to take?"

"I don't know." Bryan sat down a few inches from
his sister. "But we can't do anything until this is re-

solved. They don't want any stock being moved. They're even talking about shutting us down."

"Shutting—Bryan! You can't be serious."

Bryan's look was the only answer Lynn needed to hear. "Dee and I know we're innocent. I think, deep down, the rodeo committee believes in our innocence. But that isn't doing us much good right now."

"I know you're innocent," Lynn whispered. "I would have never sold Red to you if there'd been any question. I've been travelling with you all season. I've shipped White Moon with your stock. I wouldn't be here if—"

"Thank you."

That was all he needed to say. With those few simple words, Lynn could almost believe that the distance between them no longer existed. He was beleaguered, maybe even in need of reassurance of his worth. No matter what the circumstances between them might be, Lynn could give him that.

She reached out, took Bryan's hand and drew it to her. Their knees almost touched in the trailer's narrow confines. When Bryan sighed, she could feel his breath. She could remember the feel of his lips on hers.

But he wasn't reaching for her. Although she knew the time wasn't right, that fact frightened Lynn and gave her the desperate courage to bring his hand to her lips. She hadn't forgotten how he tasted. "Are you going to be all right?"

Now I am, he thought. Bryan's mind had been whirling with possible actions, possible arguments. He'd been aware that Lynn was in the trailer, but it had taken a minute for the impact of her presence to burrow deep inside him. Now he was aware of very little except her. "We'll survive," he said absently. "This isn't the first trouble we've had."

"I know that. But you're upset."

"Yes, I'm upset. And frustrated. The rodeo committee's seen the pictures, but no one will let us have a look at them." Bryan could have passed off her concern, boarded up his emotions and shown her no more than his professional side. But Lynn already knew things about him that no other human did. She had already claimed so much of his heart. "I take pride in the way I treat my animals." Glancing at Dee, he went on. "That's the way we run our business. I can take a lot, but questioning this ... I'd never knowingly hurt an animal."

"I understand, Bryan. Believe me, I understand."

At that moment, Bryan needed her understanding more than he needed to clear his name. Lynn and he had moved away from each other recently without his fully understanding why. But now, for a few seconds, he was close to her again.

But only for a few seconds. He'd come here because he and Dee had been promised a private meeting with the humane officials. Whatever might result from this time with Lynn would have to wait until things were settled again.

He could only pray that she would understand.

"I'm sorry, Lynn. But Dee and I—"

"Of course." Lynn got to her feet. "If there's anything I can do, let me know."

"I will," he said.

Chapter Twelve

Lynn saw Bryan briefly during the evening's performance, but there wasn't time to ask him whether anything had been resolved. Not that she needed words.
His mouth was set in a grim line; and even her first-
place finish on White Moon failed to elicit his usual
congratulations.

The spreading rumors did nothing to settle Lynn's
mind. Stories ranged from Stone Stock being a step
away from being shut down, and Bryan arrested for
some charge no one could specify, to one about how
an old boyfriend of Dee's had been trying to discredit
the business. Bryan had supposedly put the man in the
hospital and now he was back causing trouble. Lynn
didn't believed either story.

What bothered Lynn even more than the rumors,
and what they might do to Bryan's reputation, was
Dee's reaction. Her friend had hung listlessly over a
railing, staring at the action for most of the three-hour
rodeo. She ignored comments from those who tried to
engage her in conversation and seemed oblivious to
what was going on around her. Lynn had tried to draw
her out, but Dee barely acknowledged her presence.

As soon as the rodeo was over for the night, Bryan once again disappeared. That left Lynn with little to do except return to the trailer. Everyone else, it seemed, had more than enough to do. No one, she thought as she stepped inside, needed her.

Dee was already in the trailer, sitting on her bed in the dark. All thoughts of her own troubles left Lynn. "Bad news?" she asked gently.

"If you count no news as bad news—" Dee's voice caught and it was a minute before she went on. "Talk about getting hit with everything at once."

"I know. I'm sorry. Those stupid charges..." Lynn turned toward the small open window.

"What? Oh, Bryan will get to the bottom of it. Maybe not tonight and maybe not before we've been raked over the coals, but I know my brother. He doesn't given up."

"Then what's the problem?"

"Problem?" Dee's voice sounded hollow.

"You're depressed, my friend," Lynn pointed out. "Really depressed. I've never seen you this low. What's up that's more serious than you're letting on? Are you afraid they'll close down Stone Stock?"

"Close Bryan down?" Dee's question was bitter. "Not as long as that brother of mine is alive."

Lynn wished she had Dee's faith in Bryan's ability to move mountains, but even though she was in love with the man, she knew he was flesh and blood, not a miracle worker. "Then, I repeat, what's the problem?"

"The problem is . . . your brother."

"Did you talk to him again today?"

Lynn thought Dee had nodded, but in the dark she couldn't be sure. Lynn sat down, waiting. "For a few minutes," Dee said softly. "He finished in the money. He thinks he's ready for Cheyenne."

"That's wonderful, isn't it?"

"I'm happy for him."

"Don't do that." Lynn leaned froward, waiting until Dee was no longer staring at the ceiling. "I know you well enough to know you're miserable. I also know you wouldn't begrudge Bullet any success. So what is it?"

"What is it? I miss him so much it's killing me!"

Lynn's own feelings were echoed. "Oh, Dee. I'm sorry. I'm so sorry." Lynn took her friend's hand, shocked at how cold it was despite the warm trailer. "What did he say?" she asked a minute later. "Not about his riding. About you."

"He said . . ." Dee swung away from Lynn. On the foot of her bed was the bridle she'd taken off her horse less than an hour ago. Dee had been rubbing leather softener into the straps before Lynn came in; she started rubbing again. "I told him how I felt." Dee's strong fingers were engaged in the task of keeping life in a well-loved piece of equipment. "I told him I understood his commitment. That I don't want to get in his way. He'd hate me if I did, and I'd probably wind up hating myself."

"What did he say?"

"I know he loves me, Lynn. Before I left the ranch, when his injuries were almost healed we, you know, we became a lot more than friends. He told me that this is hard on him, too." Dee turned and looked out the window. "I think this being apart is harder than he thought it would be. He's not as single-minded as he thought he was."

"That would be an improvement."

Dee laughed a little. "Lynn? That's only the half of it. I did something I'm not very proud of. But there wasn't anything else I could do. I—I asked if I could join him."

Dee's ragged breathing told Lynn how hard it had been to make that request.

"What did he say?"

"He said only I could make that decision."

At least Bullet hadn't shut Dee out of his life. Still, he'd put a tremendous burden on her. "What have you decided?" It wasn't a fair question. If Dee had made up her mind, she would be packed, not working on a bridle in the dark.

For several minutes Dee didn't answer. The two women sat silently, listening to the soft rubbing sounds as Dee went on with her work. Lynn thought about the hours and hours she'd spent doing the same thing until the smell of leather and saddle soap had become a part of her. Maybe that was what Dee was doing tonight. She was getting in touch with herself, going back to her roots.

Finally Dee caught the bridle against her. She leaned over it, protecting the straps and metal. "This is part of me, you know," Dee whispered. "The life that goes with it is the only thing I've really ever wanted."

"I understand. Did you tell Bullet that?"

"No. It's insane, isn't it? Here I am, telling Bullet I don't know how I can live without him, and yet I'm afraid to let him know how vulnerable I feel. Lynn, you got away from this for a couple of years. You went out there and tasted what else the world had to offer. I've never really done that. I've never wanted to."

"What are you saying?"

"I'm saying I've always known where I wanted to live my life. I just didn't know who I wanted to live it with before."

"It's that serious?"

"It's that serious. That's why it's been so hard for me. Even if I'm with him, even if we were to get married, I'm not going to have as much of him as I want. Because I won't risk getting between him and his goal."

"His darn goal," Lynn supplied.

"All right." Although Lynn couldn't see Dee's features, she could sense her smile. "It isn't really that bad. I admire his determination. His direction. I can wait for him."

"Can you?" Lynn asked. "It isn't going to be much of a life for you traveling with him. He'll be putting The Finals before everything, and you'll know he could get hurt again. And this time you'll be there to see it."

"It isn't much of a life for me without him."

Then go, Lynn thought. But that wasn't her decision. Dee was weighing the pros and cons of committing herself to someone else's goal. "I wish I could help you," was all Lynn said.

"I wish you could, too. I'm not used to making decisions of the heart. Lynn, what would you do?"

"If I knew I loved him, I'd go to him, Dee," Lynn whispered. "We have to take chances in life."

"You did what Marc wanted you to. For a while you followed him. It didn't work out."

"No, it didn't," Lynn acknowledged. "But I learned something from the experience. I learned the difference between love and the excitement of being with someone with a line of blarney a mile long. I don't regret it, Dee. I understand myself a lot better as a result."

"Do you know what love is now?"

"We were talking about you."

"I know. I just... There's something else," Dee whispered. "You'd think, as many times as I've seen a cowboy get thrown, I'd get used to it. But that's the man I love out there. That part isn't going to be easy."

"Dee, he has to know how you feel. You can't keep something like that from him."

"I know." Dee's grip on the bridle increased. "If I go, I'll tell him."

Lynn couldn't drop the issue. It might be easier on Dee if she did, but changing the subject wouldn't help Dee find any answers. "He won't leave the circuit, Dee. No matter how scared you might be, he won't."

"I know that."

"And, Dee, if you go to him, you're going to die a little every time he rides."

The bridle slid through Dee's fingers. She stared at it, seemingly mystified by how it had gotten to the floor. Once again Lynn could hear Dee breathing. She would give anything not to have had to say those words, but they needed to be said.

"And if I don't go to him, I'll die even more."

Dee knew she was taking a great risk by becoming part of Bullet's uncertain world, but it was the only solution her heart would accept. Now that she had made her decision, she would have liked to leave immediately, but that wouldn't be fair to Bryan. She even decided not to worry Bryan with her decision, at least until after the rodeo had run its course and then, if the charges against them had been resolved, she would head for Cheyenne.

Although Dee had been hesitant to ask, Lynn assured her that she would be willing to cover for her. "I'll pitch in until Bryan can find someone permanent," she told Dee.

"Maybe that won't be necessary," Dee started. "Bullet's going to be at a lot of rodeos. As soon as he and I get things figured out, maybe I could go on working, at least on a part-time basis."

"I'm sure you and Bryan can work something out."

THE TWO HAD TO LEAVE that issue unresolved. Although it was late, Dee wanted to talk to a cowboy who had a car for sale. Alone in the trailer, Lynn was overcome by restlessness. No matter what she tried to find to do, her thoughts kept turning to Bryan. It wasn't like him to disappear after a performance. He could have gone to his foreman's trailer, but Lynn thought he would have wanted to discuss the status of the charges with Dee or her.

Finally Lynn had to admit that she wasn't handling her own company any better than Dee had handled inactivity. She was halfway out the door when she spotted Bryan standing by himself under one of the trees that dotted the grounds. Indecision kept Lynn rooted where she was.

The day had been one of the longest of Bryan's life. It wasn't just the charges; Bryan, like many rodeo contractors, had defended himself before. What had brought him out here was the reality of having been too long without Lynn. He thought he should be used to the transient nature of relationships. A long time ago he'd reconciled himself to the fact that his lifestyle and his nature didn't allow many friendships to grow too deep.

But what he felt for Lynn went far beyond friend-ship. Questioning, searching, running against emo-tional barriers of his own making was driving Bryan to distraction.

No wonder he'd been short-tempered during the meetings he'd been forced into earlier today. The hu-mane officials hadn't given him enough to sink his teeth into. How was he going to clear his name if their charges remained so vague and hypothetical pictures continued to be held over their heads? The rodeo committee was no more helpful. He'd worked with the same core group for four years now and had never given them reason to question his professionalism. And now, instead of vouching for his innocence, they'd dropped everything in his lap. Their message was simple. He had only a few hours to clear his name. If that wasn't accomplished, there would be no con-tract for next year.

What both groups had failed to comprehend was that Bryan Stone wasn't Superman. He could only do so much, only accept so much of the burden.

And tonight he wanted nothing to do with that burden. He wanted Lynn beside him. He wanted to talk, to touch, to make love, to tell her what was going on inside him and have her do the same. And what Bryan wanted to hear most was that Lynn wanted to spend the rest of her life with him.

He wanted—he wanted Lynn with him. Tonight and always. His thoughts ran so deep that he was unaware of her presence until she touched his arm.

"It's late," he said.

"I know." How right it felt talking to him. Did he have any idea how incredibly masculine he looked

leaning against the tree, his weight resting comfort-
ably in his well-worn boots?

Because the moon was nearly full, Lynn could see
the intense way Bryan was looking at her. For a moment she shrank under his gaze; then her courage returned. "You don't know any more than you did the
last time I saw you? About why the humane society
people are here, I mean?"

"No." Bryan drew out the word. Lynn felt like a
feather caught in a prairie wind. She didn't know what
she could do or say. When he spoke, the words weren't
the ones she'd wanted to hear. "You're on your way,
you know," he was telling her. "You're good. People
are starting to recognize that. As long as you have a
good horse, there's nowhere you can't go."

"I guess. White Moon's perfect. I'm in your debt
for having found her for me."

That was the last thing Bryan wanted to hear.
Maybe if he hadn't been committed to keeping a
promise to Lynn's parents, Lynn wouldn't have regained her love of racing. If she were still standing on
the sidelines looking for some direction for her life to
go, he could have held out his hand and drawn her
gently to him. But now that she was realizing her
dreams she didn't need him.

But he needed her.

Bryan knew he was risking everything, but he had
to take chances tonight. Tomorrow he might not have
time for her, and the day after that Stone Stock would
either be out of business or on its way to the next rodeo. He reached for her slowly, tentatively, giving her
time to turn away if that was what she wanted.

When she didn't, Bryan drew her against him,
drawing in her scent, her breath, the memory of nights

in each other's arms. He'd been so hungry for her in so many ways that the reality of those emotions tore through him, leaving him feeling like a newborn foal. He could do nothing except wait for her to lift her mouth to his. Then he drank her in and lost himself. She still fit against him; no matter what had gone wrong, she still fit.

The kiss that had begun as an exploration, an attempt to restore something that had been lost, took his thoughts away. Lynn pressed herself freely and completely against him, awakening a need that rocked him with its intensity. He needed to hear her low voice, needed to watch her long stride, needed to hear her speak his name.

The question, if such a fleeting and yet vital thought could be called a question, was whether she felt the same. He wanted to believe that her body was giving him the answer he needed. The tips of her breasts were pressing against him. She was breathing so deeply that the sound itself added to his arousal. And she was holding back.

Still, when he spoke, he refused to let his emotions intrude. Bryan, who had always been sure of himself, was anything but sure around Lynn Walker. He wanted to proclaim his love and ask her to be his wife, but they hadn't had enough time together for him to say and ask those things.

No. That wasn't it at all. What was stopping him was the fear that Lynn didn't want to hear what he had to say, that she might see words of love as a prison, his attempt to put an end to her dreams.

What was it that magazine reporter had said? "There was another woman a few years ago. She was really good, too. But she married some guy who tried to be her manager. After that things weren't the same for her. I don't know if she lost her drive or what, but she missed out on the chance of a lifetime.''

Bryan knew Lynn had to be the one directing her life. He wouldn't try to influence her. Try to cage her. Her happiness meant too much to him. "I'm glad you came out here," was all he could say. "It's been a long day.''

Caught in a whirlpool of emotion, needing him, wanting him, Lynn had hoped he would tell her that he loved her. She wanted to hear that he'd felt that way for a long time, but had known that certain things couldn't be rushed.

But that wasn't what he said. And her reply was no better. "Tomorrow will be, too. You have to meet with them again then, don't you? Is there anything I can do to help?''

Be there. Tell me again that you love me and let me find the strength to believe it this time. "I don't think so.'' Bryan was torn. If he continued to hold Lynn against him, he would wind up making love to her. He couldn't do that. Not daring to breathe, he pushed her away from him. The gesture tore him apart. "I have to do this alone.''

"I understand.'' He didn't want her kisses, her arms around him, her body holding nothing back. Somehow she would have to find a way to survive that knowledge. "But I'll be there if you need me.''

"Thank you.''

AFTER A SLEEPLESS NIGHT, Lynn was up before Dee. She'd pulled on her clothes so she could search for coffee, but she was still in the trailer when Bryan entered it. His message was terse. The humane society had turned its investigation over to the privately run Animal Protection Society. The Society, which took a hard line where rodeos were concerned, would be here in a half hour. They wanted someone to give them access to all the stock and that person could not be either Bryan or Dee Stone.

"They don't want anyone on my payroll talking to them," Bryan explained. "I tried to point out that no one else would know what's going on, but they're adamant. Lynn, they agreed to let you show them around. Are you willing to do it?"

"Me? But do they know?" Lynn stopped. What was she going to do, ask Bryan why his...what was she to him? And why was she acceptable when his sister wasn't?

"I just told them you've been traveling with us. They don't need to know anything else."

Of course, Lynn thought, before she agreed to Bryan's request. She barely had time to pull herself together before the two men from the society arrived, demanding first to see the calves used in the roping events. Lynn led the way to the corral, her empty stomach grumbling. Lynn hadn't expected to like the two men and, although she was trying to at least be cordial, nothing had happened to change her mind. At least they'd had enough sense to show up in working clothes, but it was obvious that they'd already judged Bryan guilty and didn't believe anything would happen today to sway their opinions. They each had a camera, and a clipboard on which they made notes.

Although they barely spoke to Lynn, she sensed that they were disappointed when they reached the calf corral. "Where are the others?" the younger of the two men asked.

"That's all the calves they brought here," Lynn explained. "The steers are beyond that trailer. The Stones try to keep them away from the crowds because they're pretty wild and given their size, they could hurt themselves if they got too excited."

"That's not what we're talking about," the man repeated. "Where are the young calves?"

"Young?" Lynn pointed to the corral she'd brought the men to. "These are the youngest. They run six hundred pounds and up. I'm sure you know that that's standard for calf roping events."

The men exchanged looks but said nothing. After taking a couple of pictures, they had Lynn take them to where the larger steers were being held. Lynn noticed that they took pictures of the water trough, but since the trough had been filled with fresh water that morning, as it was every morning, she wasn't concerned. They spent considerable time observing the broncs used in the bucking events, and the older man slipped in for a close-up shot of a half-healed barbed wire cut on one gelding's chest. Because the cut had been treated with medication that was designed to keep the flies off, Lynn had no qualms about that picture, either. The last stop was to study the bulls.

"I don't know if you'll take my word for this," Lynn said. "But the Stones don't have any bulls under fifteen hundred pounds. Bulls of thirteen hundred pounds are allowed, but I've never seen one that small. If you want to, I'll introduce you to the clowns who are working this rodeo. Ask them anything you want to. They can give you an objective opinion from someone who doesn't work for the Stones."

"I don't see what good that would do, Miss Walker," the younger of the two men said. "The clowns are in Stone's pocket, aren't they?"

Lynn groaned silently at the prospect of having to explain everything. As briefly as possible, she told the men that the clowns were independent agents who signed separate contracts with the rodeo committees, not the stock contractors. "If there's any clown who really knows Bryan and Dee," Lynn added, "it's Rusty Landers. He's worked dozens of rodeos that used Stone Stock over the years. He's not working this rodeo, but I'm sure we have his phone number."

"That won't be necessary." The two men were leaning against the fence watching the massive beasts with their huge muscles, loose hide, deadly horns. One of them reached down for a small rock and tossed it gently toward the closest bull. Although the rock hit squarely between his hooves, the creature did no more than grunt and stare at the men through tiny eyes. "Come on, you beast. Charge me," the man said.

"Why?" Lynn asked. "He doesn't hate you."

The man's laugh gave Lynn some indication of what he thought of her statement. "I've seen a lot of bulls in my life, Miss Walker. I know what their dispositions are like. In fact, I've probably been to as many rodeos as you have."

Lynn doubted that, but she wasn't here to argue with the men. "If that's the case, then you must have an understanding of their nature. They don't spend every waking hour looking for someone to maim."

"Tell that to a fallen cowboy," the other man spoke up. "Are you trying to tell me that what we see in the arena is fake?"

"Of course not." Lynn kept her eyes on the bulls. Otherwise she might give into the impulse to chuck a rock at one or both of the men with her. "But out here they're left alone. No one's trying to agitate them so why should they want to hurt us?"

"Because it's their nature, Miss Walker," the older man pointed out in a condescending tone. "Surely you've been around enough bulls to know that."

Lynn wasn't sure whether the men were simply trying to get her goat, but she couldn't sit back and let them make their misconceptions sound like fact. "I'd be mad, too, if someone buckled a flank strap around my belly, and there was a clanging bell dangling under me, and cowboys were yelling at me to make sure I get out of the chute. But . . ." Lynn pointed at a dozing bull that weighed in at over a ton. "I sure wouldn't be that sleek and well padded if I was charging around twenty-four hours a day."

Although the men took a half dozen pictures of the bulls, they didn't come up with any more stereotypical thinking about the rodeo business. They wanted to see the feed supply, the barns, even the holding pens where the animals were held prior to their events. Lynn got a perverse pleasure from watching how awkward the men were at crawling around the bucking chutes while she easily scrambled over the maze of wooden fences.

"I think that's all we're going to need you for, Miss Walker," the older man said after she'd spent close to two hours with them.

Lynn knew she was being dismissed, but she was determined to pull as much information as possible out of the men before she left. "What happens now?" she asked. "Don't you have to pass judgment in time for a decision to be made about tonight's performance?"

"Before noon." The older man glanced at his companion.

"Will you be talking to Bryan again? It bothers me that the Stones haven't been told what or who prompted this investigation or been able to see the evidence against them."

"That isn't necessary, Miss Walker. Our job, our only job, is to determine whether animal rights have been violated."

They were waiting for her to ask if they'd come to a decision, but Lynn wasn't going to give them that satisfaction. She saw her job as projecting a sense of confidence about Stone Stock. If she had no doubt that this was a humane, professionally run contract business, it just might rub off on the men. "That's fine," she told them, her voice confident. "I'm sure everyone's going to be glad to have this resolved. It's really a shame that it had to take up so much of everyone's time."

The older man had been studying his clipboard. When Lynn spoke, he looked up. "Let me ask you something, Miss Walker. If you were in my position, what would your decision be?"

Lynn answered easily. "I allow my mare to be transported with the Stone animals. She means everything to me. Without her, I'm out of business so to speak. If I had any doubts about her safety or the quality of the care they give the animals they transport, I wouldn't be here. Not that long ago, my mare somehow got out of her corral. I looked—" Lynn pressed her hand to her forehead, reliving those tense hours. "I looked everywhere. All night. Bryan was with me the whole time. When someone cares for animals, it shows. In spite of that incident, I still transport my mare with Stone Stock. I trust Bryan and his company completely."

Lynn didn't know how much impact her statement had on the men, but because the words were honest, she hoped that was how they interpreted them. She accompanied the men back to the rodeo office and then took her leave. By then the only thing on her mind was putting an end to her stomach's insistent growling.

She was able to talk one of the vendors out of a hot dog, and was trying to convince herself that she wasn't as tired of the taste as she was, when she spotted Dee. For the first time in days, her friend was smiling.

No, Dee explained, she hadn't heard anything more about the investigation, but she *had* gotten in touch with Bullet. "I think I woke him up," she laughed. "They were forever getting him to the phone and believe me, the rodeo secretary there would probably like to see me tarred and feathered after all the trouble I put her through. But it was worth it. Lynn, he sounds so happy!"

"He does?" Lynn shared her friend's smile. "Why didn't that turkey let you know that before?"

Dee shook her head. "You know how proud that brother of yours is. He wouldn't admit he needed or wanted anyone if his life depended on it. And maybe . . . I think he needed us to be apart a while for him to realize it wasn't what he wanted. And I've been thinking about my fear for his safety. If we're together, I think I can cope with that."

"Then it's all set?"

"It's all set. Bullet understands what's going on here. He said to come as soon as I can." Dee's grin grew even wider. "Oh, Lynn, you have no idea how wonderful I feel. How free. How open. I'm probably taking the biggest chance I've ever taken, but I feel here—" Dee indicated her heart "—that I'm doing the right thing. Did you know, you can hear love over the phone. Even on a long-distance call."

"You can?"

"I can. Bullet loves me. We'll work things out."

The last thing Lynn would ever try to do was tell Dee that she didn't know what her best friend was talking about. Unlike Lynn, Dee knew what was in the heart of the man she loved. But because Lynn didn't want that terrible reality to overwhelm her this morning, she guided the conversation in a safe direction. She told Dee about playing tour guide for the two officials. "I got a little carried away about my confidence in Bryan. But it's true, he does care about animals. When I think of the way he worried and searched the night White Moon was missing. Dee—"

"What?"

Lynn shook her head. Something... "That's never happened before, has it? No other animal has gotten out of the corrals."

"No."

"Then why White Moon?"

"Lynn? What are you talking about?"

"I'm not sure," Lynn muttered. It just seemed pretty strange that something like that could happen.

WHEN BRYAN FOUND HER LATER, Lynn was half watching one of the other barrel racers go through her paces, while her mind continued working at pieces of the puzzle of White Moon's disappearance. Bryan silently touched her on the arm. Then he spoke. "They want to meet with me in ten minutes."

"Do you have any idea what's going to be said?"

Bryan shook his head. "Did they seem surprised by anything they saw today?"

"It's hard to tell. Bryan, I want to attend."

"Why? There's nothing you can do."

"Maybe. Maybe not. Bryan, please."

Bryan traced a circle in the dirt. Then, grunting, he got to his feet and helped Lynn up. "They might throw you out of the meeting."

"Maybe. I'll take my chances."

THE TWO MEN LYNN HAD SHOWN around the grounds were already in the rodeo office when Bryan, Dee and Lynn entered. She hated the courtroom atmosphere. The men glared at Lynn. "This is a private meeting, Miss Walker."

"I'm aware of that." Lynn sat down, trembling a little. "However, I have something I want to say. If you don't mind, I'd like to say it now, and then if you don't feel it's relevant, I'll leave."

The older man glanced at his notes. "It won't take long?"

"Not long." Lynn took a deep breath. She could appear tentative; given the nature of her suspicions, maybe she should. But too much was at stake. She had to be aggressive. "Earlier today I mentioned that Bryan Stone shared my concerns when my mare disappeared. It was an unfortunate, frightening accident. Only—" Lynn took another breath. "—I don't believe it was an accident."

"What does this—"

"Please. I'll get to that. Yesterday I was talking to a man who reminded me of that accident. That man said something that didn't register with me then, but it does now. He brought out a point he couldn't possibly have known if he hadn't been the one to take White Moon from her corral. Only Bryan and I knew that my horse had been found on a school ground."

"Miss Walker—"

Lynn held up her hand to stop the man's question. She felt Bryan's eyes on her, but didn't risk being distracted by looking at him. "That man was Tate Carr."

"Tate Carr." The man who'd tried to interrupt Lynn a moment before was now speaking slowly.

Lynn nodded. She'd seen the man's quick blink; if the name Tate Carr didn't mean anything to him, he wouldn't be interested in something that had happened weeks ago, would he? "I don't know how he took my horse. But as for why, maybe—" Lynn turned toward Bryan "—maybe I do."

Bryan took over. It didn't take long for him to describe the run-ins between him and the clown with the drinking problem. "He was here yesterday?"

Dee spoke up. "I thought I saw him a little while ago. Wouldn't you think, if he was really here because he had reformed, as he told Lynn, that he'd want Bryan to know? You haven't seen him, have you, Bryan?"

Bryan started to shake his head, but wasn't given the opportunity to speak. The older of the two society members broke in. "We're discussing unethical charges against you, Mr. Stone, not this."

"Aren't we?" Bryan pushed himself to his feet. "I think I've been pretty patient. I understand you have a job to do. But if Tate Carr is behind your being here, I have the right to know that.''

The two men put their heads together. While they whispered between themselves, Lynn and Dee silently clasped hands. Bryan remained on his feet, his mouth grim. Once he glanced down at Lynn, but his expression gave away nothing of what he was thinking.

Finally the men were done. ''You're right, Mr. Stone. The investigation has reached the stage where there is no harm in telling you that. Yes, Mr. Carr had concerns about your operation. However. . .''

Bryan waited with his fists clenched at his sides. There was now no doubt in his mind that Tate had stolen White Moon and put Lynn through a night of hell. That angered him more than what was happening to him now.

''We have been supplied with pictures.''

''So I've heard.'' Bryan wasn't about to wait for an invitation. Before anyone could say anything, he crossed the space separating him from the men and reached for the file. He half expected to be told he had no right, and he had no intention of listening, but they remained silent.

Lynn and Dee joined him. Slowly Bryan spread out pictures: cattle standing around a dry watering trough; a couple of frightened young calves with their rumps pressed against a fence; the interior of a filthy cattle truck. ''This is the evidence against me?''

''These pictures were taken the night you arrived. At least—'' the two men exchanged glances ''—that's what we were led to believe.''

''That liar!'' Dee exclaimed.

Bryan ignored his sister. "Take a look," he said. "In the background of this shot. That's a hill. There aren't any hills here."

Lynn stabbed her finger at the picture of the water-deprived cattle. "Didn't it bother you that this picture doesn't show a single brand? What proof do you have that these are our...the Stones's cattle? And this truck. It could be any truck."

Bryan wasn't finished. He leaned forward and planted his hands on the table. "This isn't the first time this has happened this year. The other time, in Union, Oregon, things didn't get this far. I'm sure you have those records as well. Take a look at who filed the charges. You do keep track of that, don't you? See if you don't come up with the name Tate Carr."

"Tate Carr," the older Animal Protection Society officer repeated. "You're saying you've had run-ins with him before?"

"Run-ins? I'll never be able to prove it, but I'm willing to bet the business that one of his stunts nearly had me killed."

Bryan's explanation took some time. Afternoon shadows were just beginning to form when Bryan, Lynn and Dee left the rodeo grounds office. Still inside were the two men working on the report they would turn over to the humane society clearing Stone Stock of all charges. After hugging her brother, Dee broke free. She said she was going to try to get through to Bullet to let him know what had happened.

"It wasn't an accident," Lynn muttered. She and Bryan were walking aimlessly, needing to work off nervous energy. "That time the bull caught you in the chute wasn't an accident. Why didn't you say anything before this?"

"What could I say, that I found a broken cattle prod in the dust when I've outlawed the things?" Bryan gave his foreman the thumbs-up sign but didn't try to steer Lynn toward him. "I kept telling myself there wasn't anything but coincidence between BlueBoy going crazy that night and that damn thing. One of my men could have slipped it in behind my back thinking it would make his job easier and then dropped it when he thought someone might see. There still isn't any proof that Tate was behind that, but it gave those Animal Protection guys something to think about."

"When I think of what Tate almost got away with . . . Bryan, I know he was behind what happened to BlueBoy." Without thinking about it, Lynn headed toward the area where the barrel racers practiced. "When I think of what you were put through because of Tate. Why did he do something so insane?"

"I don't know, Lynn. We'll probably never know."

"I'm just so glad it's over. Now we can get back to . . ." Lynn's voice trailed off.

The charges had claimed so much of him in the past couple of days. There should have been time to spend with Lynn, but it hadn't happened; he hadn't made time. This business that was both his master and mistress had always been the main force of his life. For as long as he could remember, Bryan had been content, even happy with that. But that was before Lynn had entered his life. At least she'd come close; she hadn't really entered it.

So Bryan had his business and Lynn had her goal. No wonder they were sitting on a bale of hay just outside the barrel racing practice area talking about the confrontation, and a question of attempted murder, and horse stealing, and the dropping of the charges, and everything but what they really needed to say.

It was his fault. Even if the humane society had almost shut him down, even if Stone Stock seemed likely to become nothing more than a memory, he should have found time for her. She was the most important person in his life. But the charges had been something he could attack, something, with Lynn's help, he could get his hands on.

Lynn had blown into his life. And she would blow out again because he would never ask her to put her future aside for him.

Somehow, once she left, he would have to find a reason to go on.

But, if nothing else, he could give her some of what she'd given him. Bryan didn't want it to be here; anywhere would be better than where Lynn labored to hone her skills. The setting reminded him too much that her world didn't include him.

Lynn had a rare talent. She would see her name in lights and reap the rewards that went with that skill. He wouldn't try to stand in her way. But he needed her to know that she'd touched him.

"I couldn't have done it without you. We'd still be in there trying to clear our names if you hadn't put two and two together. I meant what I said in there. I want a restraining order against Tate Carr. I don't want him within a hundred miles of a Stone rodeo. Lynn, what you did—"

"I'm glad I could help. To think I believed Tate when he told me he'd turned over a new leaf. If he hadn't said what he did about White Moon— Where would we be if he hadn't slipped and let me know he knew where White Moon had been found?"

"Sometimes the right words come along." Stop it, Bryan warned himself; stop avoiding the truth. "I'm talked out, Lynn. I just want to put the past two days behind me. Go on with life."

"Yes." Lynn sighed. Her eyes were on the trio of barrels set up in the enclosure. "Go on with life. What a wonderful thought."

"Lynn, what are you going to do now?"

"Now? About what?"

About your life. About us. "So many things have happened to you since your father died. You've gone back on the circuit, become a top performer. I just..." Lynn should be tending to White Moon. He couldn't keep her here much longer. "There's something I think we need to talk about. It won't take long."

Lynn glanced at Bryan. "There is?"

"Do you remember what you said to me the last time we were home?"

"What?"

"It was night."

Lynn nodded, then spoke, slowly. "I—I told you I loved you."

Why was it so hard for him to speak? "I didn't know what to say to you then."

Lynn wasn't looking at him. "It was hard for me to say. I—I wasn't sure it was the right thing."

Why? Because she didn't mean the words? Because Bryan didn't want to hear the answer; he didn't ask the question. "I appreciated it. I should have been as honest."

"Honest?"

She was shaking. Bryan couldn't let her do that. He had to say the words quickly; hand her what he could of himself. "I should have told you that I loved you, too."

"You..." Lynn was shaking even more, her fingers clamped around her calves, her eyes dark caves. "Loved me."

"A little bit." Bryan made himself smile. It was the hardest thing he'd ever done, the biggest lie he'd ever told. But, because what he'd found in her eyes was rocking his foundation, Bryan buried himself in the lie. He left her free to follow her star. "It isn't serious. Nothing for you to be concerned with."

"A little bit," Lynn repeated. She was staring at him, but he couldn't see into the caverns her eyes had become.

"Nothing you need to worry about," he told her. What else could he say? Lynn had to be free. He would never tie her to him. Even if it meant lying to her about their love.

Chapter Thirteen

Lynn felt nothing. The day had become almost unbearably hot, which tended to make the animals lethargic, and the people who were charged with their care short-tempered. But word had spread quickly about the dropped charges and the collective sense of relief at the rodeo made suffering through the long afternoon more bearable for everyone.

But Lynn was wrapped in cotton. She felt nothing. She had heard only one thing.

Bryan was, or had been, a little bit in love with her...

But it wasn't anything for her to worry about. Nothing to pin hopes and dreams and a future on.

Why should she have believed it could be any different, she told herself when tears threatened. She had nothing to offer Bryan. He had his life together; he had goals. He deserved a woman with more to her name and future than a fast, strong mare.

All too soon, it was time for Lynn to prepare for her evening's ride. Other nights she'd concentrated on her makeup, her hair, her outfit. Tonight, although the white outfit turned heads, everyone who came close would note that Lynn Walker hadn't bothered to accent her deep-set eyes and there was an almost frightening depth to them. If anyone had asked, she would have told them it wasn't anything they needed to worry about. She'd been told the same thing; the words would come easily enough.

Perhaps White Moon sensed her rider's inattention, or maybe the young mare simply felt rejuvenated because the heat had lessened. Either way the mare reached deep inside for the competitive edge that her mistress was unable to share with her tonight.

White Moon ran with heart and soul. For the first five seconds, Lynn was little more than a passenger. Then the magic between her and White Moon touched her and the two of them became one. Bryan, watching when he should have been working, saw the perfect mesh between them and believed it proved he'd done right to lie to Lynn. He'd had to tell her he loved her; he couldn't have been completely dishonest with Lynn about that. He'd just described limits on his love when in truth there were none. He'd left the door open so Lynn could leave him when her time came.

As Lynn bent low over White Moon and flew past the finish line, Bryan took what she was into his heart. What Bryan did know was that tonight he loved Lynn Walker more than he'd ever loved anyone before. And because he loved her, he would never chain her to him.

Lynn accepted the congratulations that followed her run, but her praise was for White Moon, and her eyes were for Bryan. She knew that he was watching her, sitting astride his stallion, totally at home in his surroundings. For a few weeks, he'd given her a little of himself, and for that she would always be grateful.

And at least he loved her a little bit, she reminded herself. It wasn't enough; it would never be enough. But at least she had that.

And because she loved him, Lynn would leave him free to find a woman with more to offer him.

By the time she'd finished being interviewed by a television reporter and had taken care of White Moon, the bucking events had begun. Drawn to them despite what was happening inside her, Lynn took her usual perch, staring through the haze of lights and dust until she spotted Bryan. His stallion, like White Moon, had recovered from the day's heat and was filled with a restless energy that forced Bryan to handle him with unaccustomed firmness. Lynn had always been a little in awe of Stone Two. She felt more in tune with White Moon who existed only to please her; who gave everything there was to give.

Maybe it was the night. Maybe it was the residue left behind by Bryan's words to her. And maybe it was because Lynn had made a decision but hadn't yet been able to face it. Whichever it was, she found something terribly profound in the difference between the two animals. Each served its own purpose. Each was right for its master or mistress. But they weren't interchangeable because the owners were so different.

Bryan had everything. He knew who he was and where he was going. And Lynn knew that she loved Stone Two's master.

"All I can say is, I'm glad I'm not competing against you."

Dee's voice startled her, but Lynn was grateful for the distraction. She waited while Dee joined her on the fence before saying anything. "It's White Moon,"

Lynn explained. "I don't believe in making comparisons, but I don't think even Nevada Girl was that good."

"I don't know." Dee hooked her boots under a railing and gripped the one she was sitting on. "I haven't been on either horse enough to make comparisons. I know you're doing better on White Moon, but then maybe that's because you're better. You've been doing a lot of practicing."

"It's something to do."

Ignoring the wild-eyed bronc who was thundering past them, Dee focused on Lynn. "It sure looked like a lot more than just finding a way to fill the time."

"I didn't mean it like that," Lynn tried to amend. She started to explain and then stopped herself. Her thoughts were too heavy for any evasion. "When Bryan brought White Moon to me, I honestly thought I wanted to compete. I did then. I still do. But—a silver buckle? There has to be more of a purpose to life than that."

"You better believe there is." Dee shifted her weight. "I'm surprised you'd forgotten that. It's like Bryan said the other day. Keep going the way you are, and you're going to be offered some promotional contracts. There's money in those, you know. Big money."

"Money." Lynn tossed off the thought. It was no more than a word to her. "Bryan said that?"

Dee nodded. Although she was now leaning forward to watch the still bucking bronc, Dee was in no danger of losing her perch. "He doesn't think there's any limit to what you can accomplish. Play your cards right, and you'll wind up a rich woman."

"You really think so?" Why was she asking that? Lynn didn't care.

"Hey, I don't have a crystal ball. If I did, I'd know what's going to happen once I join Bullet. But the signs are there for you, kid. You know how it was for Larry Mahan and the Ferguson brothers."

Lynn had cut her teeth on stories of the careers of those rodeo immortals. She knew them by heart. "I'm hardly in their league."

"Minor point," Dee tossed off. "You have my brother in your corner. If he thinks you can do it, who are you to argue?"

Lynn didn't have anything to say to that. It warmed her to know that Bryan had given her career thought, or at least it would have if knowing that hadn't forced Lynn to face something else. Bryan was talking about her future.

A future that Lynn might or might not want.

"What's wrong?"

Lynn blinked. She tried to focus on her white jeans, but the knees were smudged with dust. Just like her relationship with Bryan, she couldn't keep that from Dee. "Too much."

Dee waited until the latest bronc ride was over before trying to make herself heard. "I kind of thought that."

"You did?" Talking with Dee was helping.

"The two of you aren't sharing the trailer anymore. And Bryan looks the way he did when Stone Two kicked him once, just after he bought him. It wasn't hard for me to add things up."

"I don't want to hurt Bryan."

"He cares for you. Something's wrong between you. He's bound to be hurt and so are you."

Lynn could understand that. She would never knowingly cause Bryan pain, but she didn't regret what they'd had. "Life doesn't turn out the way we think it's going to, does it?" Bryan was little more than a blur at the far end of the arena now. He was moving, always moving. Always moving with purpose.

"You're awfully profound tonight."

"I'm trying to be." Lynn didn't think she was going to cry, but she couldn't be sure. This was Bryan's life. The world around them was the reason for his heart to beat. Tonight Lynn loved him, even more than she had the night she'd given her heart to him.

But her heart wasn't enough. She had to have more than that to give him. "I wish life was simpler."

"You and me both, kid. What is it? Maybe I can help."

"I doubt it." The pickup riders were ready for the next cowboy to come out of the chute. The bronc's head could be seen over the top railing; his snorts rent the night air. Lynn felt the animal's anger and wished her emotions were that simple. "Dee, I don't have enough to offer."

"What?"

"I don't have enough to offer Bryan."

"Where did you get a fool idea like that?"

"Please. Don't make fun of me." Lynn had to stop talking because the bronc was in the arena, his earlier snorts of disgust now being echoed in the furious pounding of his hooves. The cowboy managed to stay on for the first three or four jumps, but before the bell sounded, the young man was sprawled in the dirt.

"Bryan has always known what he wanted out of life. He's made the business a success. And what do I have to show for my life? A horse." Lynn jabbed at her white jeans. "And an outfit I can't wear anywhere but here."

"So?"

"So Bryan has done something with his life and I haven't."

"That, my friend, is the craziest thing I've ever heard."

"Is it?" Although the pickup riders could have done the job, Bryan had ridden over to the fallen cowboy and was offering him a ride back to the fence. He leaned over, gave the cowboy a hand and easily swung him up behind him. Bryan was strong; others depended on that strength.

Lynn would never ask Bryan to carry her through life. He couldn't possibly love a woman who asked that of him.

"I can't put it into words," Lynn told Dee while they waited for the next cowboy to begin his ride. "I feel so damn inadequate around Bryan."

"Have you talked to him about the way you feel?"

"No," Lynn had to admit. "I don't have to. He said he doesn't care for me that much."

"He did what?"

At Dee's incredulous tone, Lynn tried again. "Not that exactly. He—he said he loved me a little bit."

"As in being a little bit pregnant?"

"Don't make fun of me," Lynn warned.

"I'm not making fun of either of you." Dee was glaring at her, her usually sunny face shadowed. Lynn had never felt her friend's anger directed at her before. "What I'm saying is, there's no such thing as being a little bit pregnant. And there's also no such thing as being a little bit in love."

Another cowboy came out of the chute. And after him, another. If anyone had asked her, Lynn wouldn't have been able to say whether the two had stayed on their horses or been thrown. While the bulls were being loaded into the chutes, a man with two trained Brahmas came into the arena and had them perform tricks for the audience. Lynn had never liked seeing animals used this way, but tonight they were nothing more than a blur to her in the hot, dust-hazed air.

The night smelled of sweat, cotton candy, hay, popcorn, leather and horses. The sounds that made up her world were as familiar to Lynn as the beating of her own heart. She didn't need to concentrate to hear them; even when her thoughts shut them out, they remained a part of her.

There's no such thing as being a little bit in love.

For her, that was true. Even when she'd told Bryan that what she felt for him was nothing he had to concern himself with, love had consumed all of her. And yet, she'd believed she needed to pull back, to give Bryan only part of herself. There was safety in pulling back. Safety and loneliness.

Was Dee right? Was Bryan being no more truthful than she'd been? But why? Why would he keep some of himself from her?

Lynn didn't know the answer. All she had was the need to ask Bryan. Then she'd hear the words that would either save or destroy her.

The first bull of the evening burst out of the chute with a lean cowboy clinging to him. Two seconds later the cowboy and bull had parted company, and the clowns had hurried in to divert the bull while the cowboy scrambled to safety. The second cowboy lasted a little longer, but he, too, was thrown before completing his ride. By then there were two loose bulls running in the arena, left there to entertain the fans while the next cowboy got ready for his ride.

At a signal from Bryan, a couple of handlers rode after the bulls with the intention of herding them toward the open gate that would take them out of the arena. One bull found the opening and charged through it. The second came within a few feet of the gate before sliding to a halt and whirling back into the arena.

He should have been ready. Bryan had been in this position a thousand times. He knew how quickly his stallion would respond, how little time it took Stone Two to go from standing still to a full gallop.

But tonight Bryan Stone's mind was on the white-clad woman perched on a wooden fence above the action. He was surrounded by heat and dust, pounding hooves and scrambling bodies. She was quiet, peace, self-containment. He was all nervous energy and too much thinking.

"Bryan!" one of the handlers yelled as Stone Two took off after the escaping bull. Despite the warning, Bryan was pulled off balance by Stone Two's charge. He grabbed the saddle horn and would have easily righted himself if his stallion hadn't turned sharply in an attempt to keep up with the bull. Once again Bryan had to concentrate on staying in the saddle instead of anticipating his mount's next movement.

Stone Two was running low to the ground, boxing
the bull into a corner as he'd been taught. The horse
expected his master to either lasso the bull or ask him
to herd it toward the gate. Bryan opted to give the bull
one more chance to find the opening before reaching
for his rope, but he was still half a heartbeat behind
Stone Two. He wasn't timed to his stallion.

But the bull was.

Instead of seeking an escape route, the bull known
as Number Thirteen turned and faced his attacker.
Stone Two slid to a stop, dragging his haunches on the
ground. Bryan was thrown forward and almost unseated. He'd almost regained his seat when Number
Thirteen charged. In an instinct that went no further
than self-preservation, Stone Two threw his body
sideways and out of the way of those deadly horns.
The sudden, violent movement threw Bryan out of the
saddle.

He should have hit the ground. Any other time he
would have landed in an inglorious heap in the dust,
but Number Thirteen was too close. As he fell, Bryan
bounced off the bull's hump. His head was only inches
from the deadly horns. The reality of his situation
buried itself deep in Bryan, and like his stallion, his
only thoughts were of self-preservation.

As he landed, Bryan drew his arms and legs under
him. His body was curled into a tight protective ball
and he was rolling away among the legs of both his
horse and the enraged bull. He managed to roll toward Stone Two's dancing hooves, but Number Thirteen had anticipated his move.

Bryan felt the horns. He froze, waiting for the pain,
waiting maybe for death.

But spearing his victim wasn't Number Thirteen's way. Instead, he slid his horns under Bryan and lifted him over his head as easily as a fork lift hefts a bale of hay. Things happened so rapidly that Bryan barely had time to understand that he was no longer on the ground. Now he was flying through the air, tossed aloft by the angry bull. Bryan remained tucked into a ball, protecting his head and vital organs. Still, when he hit the bull's back, the impact on his right side knocked the breath from him. And as he slid over the bull's side, a hoof caught Bryan on the back of his head.

THE CLOWNS AND BULL HANDLERS raced in to divert Number Thirteen and guide the bull as he bucked his way to the gate. Then all eyes were on the limp form in one corner of the arena, and on the woman in white who was running toward him.

Lynn had seen Bryan unseated, seen him hit the ground, seen Number Thirteen throw him into the air. She had jumped from her perch and was racing along the inner side of the arena almost before Bryan hit the ground again. She tried not to think about the way he lay so still in the dust, but she had Dee's scream to spur her on.

BRYAN MOVED. He shouldn't be here. There was dust in his mouth; sweat soaked his shirt; breathing was damn hard. Although he fought for clarity, all Bryan could feel was the pain at the back of his head. Still, he knew it wasn't safe to remain where he was.

Someone was touching him. He smelled more sweat and focused on a clown's painted face. "Don't move," Jagger was saying. "Not yet."

"The hell." Pushing away the clown's restraining hand, Bryan managed to get his legs under him. He'd rocked onto his knees and was trying to straighten his back when he heard another voice.

"Don't, Bryan. Not yet."

Lynn. Bryan looked up. She was little more than a white blur in a world outlined in pain. But he could stand for her. He had to. Still, when she placed her hands under his armpits and gave him support, he accepted her help. His legs felt like they belonged to a baby. His equilibrium was shot to hell. His head felt as if it had been left in the middle of a base drum too long. But at least he was standing. Lynn didn't have to see him on hands and knees.

Bryan! His name tore through Lynn, but she didn't give the word life. It was her turn to be the strong one. If she cried or screamed or let Bryan know how much she hated seeing him like this, they might never talk about anything else. And even with dust covering him and his sweat turning that dust into mud, he was the most superb man she'd ever known.

Bryan let her help him walk to the loading chutes. Someone opened the gate to the chute Number Thirteen had come out of and then closed it behind them to give them privacy. They were, if nothing else, alone. The fans could no longer see them and the bull handlers, after assuring themselves that their boss was going to be all right, were so busy readying the bull in the end chute that they had no time to waste on the quiet couple standing in the trampled sawdust.

"I don't know what happened," Bryan tried. His
throat was parched, but he felt alive. Lynn hadn't left
his side.

"I'll tell you later." She released him slowly, carefully, before touching the back of his head where a
large lump was forming. Silently she pulled the white
scarf from around her throat and used it to dab at the
blood streaking his hair. "You should get that X-
rayed."

"Later. Lynn, I'm sorry."

Bryan swayed and caught his hand to his side but
needed no help regaining his balance.

Concerned, Lynn pulled his shirt out of his jeans
and opened the tiny pearl snaps. A bruise was forming from armpit to waist.

"I didn't want you to see that," Bryan said.

"What didn't you want me to see?" Lynn asked,
filled with both anger and love. "That you're human? That there's danger in what you do? Don't you
think I know that?"

Bryan tried to shake his head. He wound up having
to reach for Lynn. When she led him to a fence, he
leaned against it. His arm was still looped over her
shoulder. His body pressed down on her. Lynn didn't
see his weight as a burden, but as affirmation of how
much they'd come to need each other. "I don't
know," Bryan said vaguely as if he were having trouble following the conversation. "Heather hated that
part of my job."

"Heather isn't here."

He'd hurt her. That was the last thing Bryan wanted
to do. And yet he believed he had to continue. "She

couldn't understand why I took chances. She wanted me to be careful."

"I'd like that, too, Bryan," Lynn said quietly, after a silence that went on so long that it frightened him. "I don't like being afraid. But I'd never ask you to change what you do."

Despite the pounding in his head, Bryan forced himself to concentrate. "You'd never want me to do something else?" He wondered if she understood that, for her, he would change his life.

"What else would you do, Bryan?"

He didn't know. The only thing that was clear to him tonight was that the woman he loved had helped him out of a dusty arena and was standing with him in an empty bucking chute with angry bulls on either side of them. This was his world; the only one he'd ever known or considered. And Lynn Walker was here sharing it with him. "I'd do whatever you wanted me to, Lynn."

Whatever she wanted. For a moment it was Lynn who needed to be supported. A man who was only a little bit in love with a woman would never say that.

Lynn had to turn away to hide the tears. As she did, her eyes focused on the rodeo arena spreading out beyond them. The bull in the end chute had charged into the arena. His wild bucking took him from one end of the oval to the other, but the cowboy riding him was strong enough and lucky enough to be able to stay with him. As long as there were bulls in the holding pen beyond, there was only one way for Bryan and Lynn to leave their momentary haven. They would have to go out into the arena again. They would have to let that dusty space absorb them. Lynn didn't have to look at herself to know that her once-white outfit would never be the same again.

She didn't care.

"I want what makes you happy, Bryan."

Was she actually saying that? Bryan wanted, with all his heart, to believe the tone he heard in her voice. He had to be sure. "What about you?" he asked. "What about what you want out of life? Lynn, you have dreams. Promise. A chance at the brass ring."

"I'm not my brother," she told him. "Making it to The Finals isn't as important to me as I thought it was."

"Don't give up your dreams, Lynn."

"Dreams?" Lynn was vulnerable, more vulnerable than Bryan had been when Number Thirteen hooked his horns under him. "I have more than one dream, Bryan. More than one thing I want out of life. I'm good at barrel racing. I found that out, and that does something for me that I love. But racing on White Moon isn't the only thing I want out of life." Would he see through her now? Lynn feared that Bryan would hear her words, and reaffirm what he already knew about how little she had to offer. She had only this limited and now unfulfilling goal she'd set for herself.

"What else do you want, Lynn?"

There was only one answer she could give him. "You."

Bryan's breathing deepened. "Me?"

"Don't do this to me, Bryan," Lynn begged. Bryan's eyes had been alive a thousand years. He was a link for her between past and future. Her past and the only future she wanted.

Bryan. She made his name sound like a loving caress. Maybe he had been wrong. He'd made himself believe that her goal in life could only be accomplished on a horse's back. But that wasn't what she was saying.

"I don't know what you want me to say," he started. That wasn't good enough. He couldn't dismiss what he needed to do. And say. "I wanted you to be free to go where you wanted, do what you needed. I told myself I wasn't going to tie you down."

"Maybe I want to be with you. Maybe I want more than I had," Lynn whispered.

Bryan had to ignore her quiet plea. Otherwise he would never finish what had to be said. "I didn't know, Lynn. That's why I didn't tell you how I really felt."

Lynn's eyes asked a million questions, but she said nothing.

"I didn't let you know how much I love you."

Lynn covered his hand with her own and trembled. "Why?"

"Because this is my life, Lynn." Bryan nodded to indicate their surroundings. "You left this once before. I thought you would leave again."

"Did I ever say I wanted to?"

"No," Bryan had to admit. "But when I found White Moon, I thought I'd given you the freedom to do what you wanted with your life. Listen to me," he went on quickly when she opened her mouth to speak. "You have talent, Lynn. If you commit yourself to it, the way Bullet has done, you'll make it to the top."

"I told you, I'm not Bullet."

"I know that, now." Another bull was doing his devil's dance in the arena. Bryan felt the ground vibrate, but he didn't take his eyes off Lynn. "I'm asking you to forgive me."

Bryan was asking her to forgive him. It should be her begging him to understand that she'd had doubts and fears and insecurities that had kept her silent. Soon she would do that. But he'd told her something that meant more to her than all the money and glory in the world. He'd said he loved her. Not a little. Not with reservations.

Bryan Stone loved her.

And Lynn loved him—his body, his hand on her cheek, his ageless eyes, his mind, his passion and compassion for life.

Maybe some of the handlers were watching them. Maybe Dee was a silent witness to what was going on in the bucking chute. Lynn didn't care. She had to feel Bryan's mouth against hers, his body molding itself to hers. And in their embrace, Lynn believed, they would find the answer they'd waited a lifetime for.

Bryan's mouth was full of passion and sweet fulfillment. A home and a haven.

Lynn wanted, for the rest of her life, to be able to reach out and always find him there. If she was beside him, and she could now imagine no other life, they would always have time for a glance, a smile, a touch. Their separate commitments couldn't take that from them. And when night came, they would have a great deal more.

"I love you, Bryan Stone."

A shudder passed through Bryan, but he stilled it so quickly that Lynn thought she might have imagined it.

"Is it something for me to concern myself with?" he asked.

"Oh yes," she answered. And despite the shadows surrounding them and the bright overhead lights trying to invade their world, Lynn was able to read Bryan's every thought, every emotion. "It's something for you to concern yourself with for the rest of your life."

"No reservations?"

"None. I'll always love you, Bryan. Nothing..." Lynn had allowed Bryan to push her away while he searched her eyes. Now she moved into his embrace again. "Nothing will ever change that."

Epilogue

It was cold in Las Vegas that December evening. Puffs of white billowed around the horses' nostrils.

Lynn, clad entirely in white as had become her trademark, guided White Moon along the wooden fencing. She kept her eyes downcast to counter the effect of the glaring overhead lights, trusting that her mare would keep pace with Stone Two.

Beside her, Bryan was watching the loading of his bucking stock. He'd allowed Lynn to select a new midnight-blue shirt for him to wear for The Finals, but he was unaware of the handsome figure he cut astride his restless stallion. But he was aware that tonight he would be showcasing the finest of his bucking stock in this, the World Series of rodeoing.

He was also aware of his bride riding beside him.

Lynn lifted her hat when she saw Dee carrying a flank strap to the chutes. Dee waved back. "I saw Bullet a few minutes ago," Lynn told Bryan. "He's pretty calm. I think your sister is nervous enough for both of them."

Bryan looked through an opening in the fencing to assure himself that a bucking saddle was being cinched correctly. "He's here by the skin of his teeth, you know. But he'd be among the top two or three if he hadn't had to lay out those weeks."

"He'll do all right." Lynn would have liked to say more, but the bucking events were about to begin. The air felt electric. Despite the cold, the fans sensed that something special was going to happen tonight, and that they were going to be part of that. Network television cameras zoomed in on the cowboys and those responsible for keeping the rodeo running smoothly. Lynn absorbed the electricity, the sense of anticipation, the feeling that tonight was destined to take its place in history.

And yet, as much as tonight represented the goal she and Bryan had been aiming toward for months, it paled in comparison to what had happened that hot night in Salinas.

Despite the need to keep White Moon out of the way of any bucking broncs, Lynn was unable to keep her eyes off her husband. They'd been able to carve out forty-eight hours of freedom last month and they'd used it to drive back to Harney county for their wedding. Dee, Lynn's bridesmaid, had wept through the ceremony. Her tears had come from her joy for Lynn and from wanting the same joy for herself. Tonight Dee was wearing a diamond herself. And as soon as The Finals were over, there would be another eastern Oregon wedding.

A flashbulb went off nearby, startling White Moon and causing the mare to rear. Lynn easily kept her balance, already reaching out to comfort White Moon before the horse's front hooves were back on the ground.

Bryan moved closer, using Stone Two as a buffer between Lynn and whoever had taken the picture. "You were good tonight," he told her. "Second place is great for your first finals."

"It is, isn't it? Not that Bullet would be happy with that."

"You don't mind not taking first?"

This wasn't the first time Lynn had been asked that question, but this time she cared how her answer was received. "I'm disappointed. I won't deny that," she told him. "But I did my best. I'm proud of that."

Bryan reached out his hand and Lynn gladly placed hers in it. For a moment they remained side by side, the world swirling around them forgotten. Last night, when Bryan had been so busy he hadn't come to bed until almost dawn, Lynn had told herself that the honeymoon was over. Reality had once again intruded.

But all it had taken to bring back the magic was for Bryan to take her hand. That was all it would ever take.

"I love you," he whispered. "I just want you to know that."

"I do know," Lynn whispered back. Expertly, the two backed their horses as a couple of pickup riders rode by. The announcer was winding up his spiel. In a few seconds the first bronc rider would be coming out of the gate.

Despite her desire to be alone with Bryan, Lynn knew that she was where she belonged. The barrel racing event was over. As Bryan Stone's wife and now as his business partner, she had taken her rightful place inside the arena. No longer did she have to wait outside, an onlooker, while Bryan worked.

Lynn squeezed Bryan's hand and let him go. He glanced over at her, smiling, and she smiled back. ''I love you,'' she said.

Home. This was home.

Harney county would be home as soon as The Finals were over. And then, in a few short weeks, the road would claim them again.

But it didn't matter where they were, whether lights shone down on them or they were alone on rolling pastures. As long as Bryan was with her, there would be peace in Lynn Stone's heart.

She could no longer remember the restlessness that had taken her away from Walker Ranch.

It hadn't been the right place to live she'd been looking for. It hadn't been another life-style or even the right horse.

It had been the right man.

And she had found him.

H A R L E Q U I N
American Romance

COMING NEXT MONTH

#309 SAVING GRACE by Anne McAllister

Cameron McClellan wasn't sure what he expected from his month-long
vacation at Gull Cottage—a break from business, carefree days with his
son, maybe even a chance to recapture his own youth. But when he
arrived to find a great big bed with a nubile blond woman in it, he found
new meaning to the question "Who's been sleeping in my bed?" Don't
miss the final book in the Gull Cottage trilogy.

#310 CODE OF SILENCE by Linda Randall Wisdom

For three years Anne Sinclair had been running from the law, changing
her name, her appearance, her address. Then she came to Dunson,
Montana, where her daughter made friends and Anne tried to make a
home. Her fear prevented her from trusting anyone, especially Dunson's
sheriff. Yet Anne was attracted to Travis Hunter—an attraction that could
be her downfall.

#311 GLASS HOUSES by Anne Stuart

All that stood between Michael Dubrovnik and the creation of Dubrovnik
Plaza was Glass House and its obstinate owner, Laura de Kelsey
Winston. Laura had the colossal gall to challenge the most powerful and
feared man in Manhattan. Michael thrived on challenges and welcomed a
battle of wills. And this was one battle he was going to love.

#312 ISLAND MAGIC by Laurel Pace

Vaness Dorsey's visit to Parloe Island was meant to be a temporary
respite before she resumed her job hunt and got on with her life. But
Great-aunt Charlotte's rambling house needed tender loving care and the
South Carolina island needed someone to protect its beauty. But the most
compelling reason to stay on was Dr. Taylor Bowen. For he understood
Vanessa's need—to belong, to care, to love.

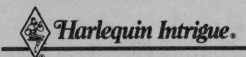

Harlequin Regency Romance™

Romance the way it was *always* meant to be!

The time is 1811, when a Regent Prince rules the empire. The place is London, the glittering capital where rakish dukes and dazzling debutantes scheme and flirt in a dangerously exciting game. Where marriage is the passport to wealth and power, yet every girl hopes secretly for love....

Welcome to Harlequin Regency Romance where reading is an adventure and romance is *not* just a thing of the past! Two delightful books a month.

Available wherever Harlequin Books are sold.

You'll flip . . . your pages won't!
Read paperbacks *hands-free* with

Book Mate · I

The perfect "mate" for all your romance paperbacks

**Traveling • Vacationing • At Work • In Bed • Studying
• Cooking • Eating**

Perfect size for all standard paperbacks, this wonderful invention makes reading a pure pleasure! Ingenious design holds paperback books OPEN and FLAT so even wind can't ruffle pages — leaves your hands free to do other things. Reinforced, wipe-clean vinyl-covered holder flexes to let you turn pages without undoing the strap . . . supports paperbacks so well, they have the strength of hardcovers!

Pages turn WITHOUT opening the strap

SEE-THROUGH STRAP

Reinforced back stays flat

Built in bookmark

BOOK MARK

BACK COVER HOLDING STRIP

10 x 7¼ opened
Snaps closed for easy carrying, too

Harlequin American Romance®

SUMMER.

The sun, the surf, the sand...

One relaxing month by the sea was all Zoe, Diana and Gracie ever expected from their four-week stays at Gull Cottage, the luxurious East Hampton mansion. They never thought they'd soon be sharing those long summer days—or hot summer nights—with a special man. They never thought that what they found at the beach would change their lives forever. But as Boris, Gull Cottage's resident mynah bird said: "Beware of summer romances...."

Join Zoe, Diana and Gracie for the summer of their lives. Don't miss the GULL COTTAGE trilogy in American Romance: #301 *Charmed Circle* by Robin Francis (July 1989), #305 *Mother Knows Best* by Barbara Bretton (August 1989) and #309 *Saving Grace* by Anne McAllister (September 1989).

GULL COTTAGE—because a month can be the start of forever...